Odd Fellows:
The Smell of Money

By Janet Kole
© 2016

This is a work of fiction. Any resemblance of the characters to real people, living or dead, is purely coincidental.

The Philadelphia I describe is not wholly realistic. I've made some changes to the geography to facilitate the story.

The legal issues that arise in this story are simplified and so not completely accurate. Also, as most lawyers know, the law changes so quickly it can make your head spin. As for the practice of law I describe, as practiced in a big firm, it is only a slight exaggeration.

Cover art: Olivia Coren
Publisher: Vinson Books, a division of VinsonPhillipPress

"An Odd Fellow bases his thoughts and actions on healthy philosophical principles. He believes that life is a commitment to improve and elevate the character of humanity through service and example. He is humble in a way that he never boasts about himself. He knows and accepts his strengths and weaknesses and keeps away from badmouthing people and making unreasonable allegations. He understands that certain things in life are unavoidable. He is aware of the vanity of earthly things, the frailty and inevitable decay of human life and the fact that wealth has no power to stop the sureness of eventual death. He then asks the question, "How am I going to spend my life?""
Source: The Independent Order of Odd Fellows, IOOF website.

For Wendy and Gabe, with love of course

PREFACE

I used to be surprised and amazed at how many different ways there are for human beings to drive each other crazy. I've come to be even more amazed at how many people there are in the world who are evil. I do believe in evil.

When I met the man who called himself Larry Evans, my view on the nature of evil was shaken. He was violent. He was a killer.

It turned out that I was lucky I met him.

The name "Odd Fellows" arose because, in smaller towns and villages, there were too few Fellows in the same trade to form a local Guild. The Fellows from a number of trades therefore joined together to form a local Guild of Fellows from an assortment of different trades, the Odd Fellows.

Wikipedia

Chapter One

The man wearing cowboy boots watched as the grey mare browsed through the pile of alfalfa. She chewed thoughtfully. He leaned against a fence post, waiting. The air was still. He could smell freshly cut onion grass from a neighbor's field.

He didn't have to wait long. The mare began to shudder. She tossed her head, back and forth. She moved on shaky legs to her water trough, and began to dip her nose into the water, then almost her entire head. She pulled her head from the trough, took a breath, put her muzzle back into the water. Her eyes rolled up in her head in panic.

The man turned around and walked through a gate in the fence. She probably had only a few hours to live. He didn't need to watch the death throes. He'd be back to be sure she was dead.

The experiment had proved interesting. The knowledge would come in handy.

Chapter Two

I was surprised to receive a call from a headhunter. I've been a partner at my law firm for so many years I'm almost retired. It seemed odd to me that any other firm would want someone as elderly as I.

"This firm would be perfect for you," said Catherine King, the so-called "executive search consultant."

"The firm I'm in is perfect for me," I said. "And I'm almost out of here."

"This firm is an Arizona firm that is trying to make inroads into the east. You would head up the Philadelphia office. You don't need to service clients. You would hire lawyers, hire administrators, run the east coast office."

"Now I know this is a dream," I said. "There is no firm in the universe that wants a lawyer without a book of business."

"Believe me, this firm is different," she said. "Check out their website. They're fun. They're not all about making money."

"If that's true, I'll eat my hat," I said. Of course, I don't wear a hat. "And if that's true, they're probably going down the tubes."

Catherine laughed. "You're a crusty old bastard, aren't you?"

I almost took offense, but didn't.

"Listen, my dear," I said, "I'm very flattered, but it seems like an awful lot of work for someone who's looking forward to puttering with my boats full time."

"Jack, do me a favor," she said. "Just think about it. This is a match made in heaven. Believe me."

I protested several more times, but Catherine convinced me to let her call me in a few days to get my final answer.

I got up from my desk, and stretched, put on my suit jacket, and walked out to my secretary's desk. Marion was ready with a handful of pink telephone message slips.

"You could use voicemail like everyone else," she said.

"Then there's no personal touch," I said.

"But if I'm feeling crabby, my personal touch isn't as good as good old voicemail," she said.

"You're never crabby," I said.

"Oh, right," she said. She handed me the slips.

Right at the top was a message from a client of the firm, Stanley Barnard. His mother had hired me years ago to handle what we called at the firm "a small personal matter." He had been arrested for buying a gram of cocaine from an undercover officer. I was able to get him into a special program for rich white kids that held the criminal charges in abeyance until he successfully completed rehab. If he then remained without a blemish on his record for the next year, the charges would be expunged. He was now a very rich white man, and his loyalty to the firm had been unwavering. We handled everything for him and his family.

"Stanley has called you several times," Marion said. Then she made a "chi-ching" sound. I think she was trying to tell me that my immediate attention to Stanley would benefit the firm financially.

"I'll call him right now," I said. Team player, that's me.

I hadn't liked Stanley much when he was a kid. I didn't like him any better now. He was an addict, but he had managed not to get arrested for any drug-related offenses in all the years since his initial arrest. His current addictions took the form of overeating and gambling. Both of these addictions were legal, so he had no need for my services in the criminal arena.

When I called the number on the pink slip, he answered immediately. It appeared to be his cell phone.

"Stanley," I said. "What's going on?"

"Jack, I need your help. My old lady is driving me crazy."

I was momentarily puzzled. I thought Stanley's marriage at least was a good one, with his wife supporting his every whim. She was also very pretty. Surely he didn't want a divorce lawyer?

"She wants to continue as President of the company," Stanley said. "She's 93 years old, for Chrissake."

Now it became clear that he was, in fact, referring to his "old" lady, his mother. The woman who had helped him stay out of the court system by hiring me at an exorbitant fee.

"Why don't you come to see me..." I said. Stanley stopped me.

"Jack, come out here. I want you to see for yourself what's going on."

When Stanley said "out here," he was referring to the headquarters of his family company, started by his mother as a small hardware store and now a conglomerate made up of hardware-related companies, including manufacturers of esoteric objects like night vision goggles. The company was still in its old location, at the edge of the Delaware River, next to garbage transfer stations and a chemical company. The hardware store was still in existence. Stanley and his family kept it operating to show that they had never really left their roots.

I agreed to meet him the next morning. I couldn't tell if he needed a litigator, an estates lawyer or a family lawyer, but presumably I'd find out. Even though I didn't like Stanley very much, I thought I'd enjoy a field trip to the hardware store.

And it turned out to be very interesting.

Chapter Three

The man with the cowboy boots buried the gray mare in one of his back fields using a bulldozer. He enjoyed using heavy machinery. Since he was a kid, he had liked to play with trucks and earth-moving equipment. As a grown man, he felt fulfilled every time he got behind the controls of one of these behemoths.

When he had finished digging the hole, he rolled the mare into it, along with the remaining alfalfa hay. He shoveled the dirt back into the hole, and ran the dozer back and forth a few times over the grave so it would settle back down to the level of the surrounding earth. Then he spread some dirt over the area the mare had fouled, with diarrhea and vomit, until it could no longer be seen or smelled.

He left the dozer in the field and headed back to his cabin. He had accomplished his goal for the week. When he wasn't working, he believed he needed to keep sharp. He needed to explore options. He liked having choices. When it came to eliminating problems, there was no "one size fits all." He thought he was probably the most flexible and creative practitioner of his craft in the contiguous states. And he wanted it to stay that way.

As he entered the cabin, his cell phone rang.

"What?" he said.

"You're needed," a familiar voice said. "Lucrative job, for both of us."

"Do I need to write anything down?"

"Just get yourself to Philadelphia. By tomorrow."

"Who am I?" said the man with the cowboy boots.

"Don't get existential on me," said the voice, and laughed.

"What the hell are you talking about?"

"Never mind. Why don't you check into the Wycliff hotel as Larry Evans. Your IDs will be waiting for you in an envelope at the desk. You can be a cowboy type if you want. Just not an actual cowboy."

The new Larry Evans shut off his cell. He didn't like small talk or jokes when he was working. He looked up bus schedules on his computer. He could make it to Philadelphia in 18 hours on Greyhound. He opened his closet and took out the suitcase he always kept packed. He'd never been to Philadelphia, but it didn't matter to him one way or the other. He had no idea what he was going to be asked to do. That didn't matter to him, either. He had everything he needed, most of it in his head.

Chapter Four

The next day I presented myself at Barnard Hardware Corporation at 9 a.m. sharp. The parking lot was empty, except for a white Cadillac. The river was quiet. I saw no river traffic. A great black-backed gull stood on a railing at the water's edge.

I rang the bell on the front door, which was locked. I heard brisk footsteps. A wizened woman opened the door to me, and when she saw me, her face broke into a smile.

"Hot diggity! Jack Morgenthau!" she said, and took my hand in one wrinkled paw.

I hadn't heard that saying in some time, but I realized it was an expression of pleasure.

"Mrs. Barnard," I said.

"Come in, come in," she said. "What brings you here?"

"I'm meeting Stanley," I said.

"You'll be waiting for a while," she said. She motioned me back into her office, which overlooked the parking lot and then the river.

"I see you still get in early," I said.

She laughed. "Even earlier now that I hardly sleep."

She sat down behind her desk, and I had a chance to really look at her. She had bleached blonde hair in an outdated pouf, which surprised me because she always looked so well put together. She used to wear her blonde hair in a bun. She was always what people in her day called "a looker." At 93, she still was. Except for the hair.

She caught me looking at her hair. She pointed a painted fingernail to her head.

"A wig," she said. "At my age, having your own hair is almost as hard as having your own teeth."

She smiled. "These aren't my originals, either."

It was hard to know how to respond. She saved me the trouble.

"You don't have to say anything, Jack. Old age is what it is."

I heard the front door open, and slow footsteps head toward the back office.

"There's nothing wrong with my hearing, though. And those fat footsteps belong to Stanley."

She paused to shake her head.

"My son just burns me up. He's a big lump of negativity. He's gotten so fat I call him Your Bulkiness."

Before I could say anything, Stanley loomed in the office doorway.

"Jack?" Stanley said. He was out of breath. "What are you doing in here?"

"You and I were supposed to meet this morning," I said.

"I know. What are you doing with my mother?"

"Oh, don't be so paranoid," his mother said. "We were just visiting."

"Come into my office," Stanley said.

I stood. "It was very nice having a chance to chat," I said.

She smiled at me again, this time very broadly, with the teeth that were not her originals, making me think of the wolf in the little red riding hood story.

Stanley was using a cane, and walking extremely slowly. He paused for breath every few steps. He had become obese since the last time I saw him. I kept my face neutral, but I was shocked at his appearance. I almost tripped on his heels; I had to hold myself back from passing him.

We finally entered his office. "Close the door," he said, as he moved slowly behind his desk. He was wheezing.

"Here's what gets me," he said. "She still thinks she runs the company."

"What does she do while she's here?" I said.

"I have no idea. She sits behind her desk and shuffles papers. She talks on the phone. She's not doing company work, I'm sure of that."

"How can you be sure?" I said.

He watched me for a few moments.

"I've bugged her office," he said.

"What?"

"I had a professional come in and bug her office. I told him I was worried she had Alzheimers."

I decided not to bring up the issue of whether what he had done was legal. It might have been.

"Does she?"

"Probably not," he said. "But I know her calls are all personal."

"You didn't bug her phone, did you?"

"No, but, you know, you can tell from one side of a conversation whether it's personal."

My heart started beating normally again. Sometimes, clients can get themselves into huge trouble. At least he hadn't broken any wiretap laws.

"Jack, you have to help me. I have a huge business to run, and she's taking up too much of my time."

"I'm having a hard time understanding, Stanley," I said. "If she's just sitting there doing nothing, how can she take up too much of your time?"

"She talks to the employees. When visitors come—like you—she talks to them. It's bad for morale."

"I would think it helps morale to have the founder still in the office, chatting with people."

"It undermines my authority."

I stared at Stanley, with his triple chin and bald head. I mentally compared his bemused face with the beautiful elderly woman's that had greeted me at the door. I could indeed see how people trusted her and not him.

"She insults me in front of the staff. She insults me when we're by ourselves. I want her out of here."

"She's still a shareholder," I said. "I don't really see how you can make her leave."

What I didn't mention was that his mother owned 51% of the company. Stanley knew it all too well.

"I want control of the company," he said.

"When your mother dies, you will have the majority of the shares," I said.

"That's what she says, but I don't trust her. She can change her will anytime."

"It's not just her will," I said. "The shareholders' agreement provides for that. Upon her death, you will own 51% of the shares."

"But don't you see?" Stanley said. "She will never die! She's the devil."

His face had turned a bright red. His neck was purple. I feared for his heart.

"Stanley," I said. "I have always represented all of you—your mother, the company, and you. If there's a problem brewing, I have to bow out. If I represented any of you, there would be a conflict of interest."

"You mean you won't help me?"

"I can't help you, ethically. You'll need to find a lawyer. And if your mother resists whatever you want to do, she'll also need to find another lawyer."

"This is unbelievable," Stanley said. "After all the money we've poured into your firm."

I started to say something. Stanley beat me to it.

"Get out," he said.

I left his office. I was sorry that there was a conflict and I could no longer be involved. I assumed I would never deal with the company or its principals again. As it turned out, their shenanigans sucked me into a morass I couldn't avoid.

Chapter Five

Larry Evans got off at the Philadelphia bus terminal, aching in every limb. Had it not been for the anonymity of the bus, he would have taken some speedier form of transportation. He put down his suitcase, placed it between his legs, and stretched as much of his torso as he could.

Bus stations in general are scuzzy, beaten looking buildings, but this one was one of the worst. A dark tunnel at the entrance also featured a dollar store and a bar, both lit with neon signs. Many people left a bus at the Philadelphia bus station fearing for their lives, in a panic. Larry Evans barely noticed his surroundings. He headed for the street to hail a cab.

"Wycliff hotel," he said to the cabby. As the cab moved from the bus station and its environs towards the Wycliff, even Evans began to notice a change in atmosphere. By the time the cab pulled up to the hotel entrance, on Rittenhouse Square, Evans saw why he couldn't be a cowboy. Just cowboy-like. The hotel was for the rich, if not for the famous.

He paid for the cab, and grabbed his suitcase, ignoring the bellman who attempted to help. He checked in, asked for his messages, and went to his room. He declined again the services of the bellman. He was polite but firm.

A message light was blinking on the room phone.

He opened the envelope that had been left for him. There was an Arizona driver's license with his

Larry Evans identity. There was a small pile of cash in fifties. He counted it. Five thousand dollars. And there was an American Express gold card in the name of Larry Evans.

He put these items into his pockets. He never carried a wallet. He might need a money clip for this much cash.

He was starved. He picked up the phone, and ignored the stuttering sound that meant he had a message. He called room service, and ordered himself a steak, rare. Then he listened to his message. He recognized the voice.

"Hi, Larry. I'm assuming you made it in ok. I'll call you on your cell at three p.m. eastern time."

He erased the message, and checked the time on the hotel room clock. He had an hour to eat before the call, assuming the hotel produced his meal in a timely fashion. He went to the minibar, and extracted a beer. That would help. Nothing like a beer to fill you up.

He thought about the grey mare. He had purchased her from a knacker, saved her life just long enough to kill her. The knacker thought he was a sentimental slob who loved animals. In truth, he hardly noticed animals. For that matter, he really hardly thought about any living creatures. But he did mull over the mare's death. Although the mare had not died quickly, he thought the cause of death would likely be untraceable. Undoubtedly, he would be placed in a situation where his experiment would prove useful.

A knock at the door brought his meat, bloody rare and smelling like heaven. He tipped the waiter, shooed him away, and sat down to destroy his meal.

Chapter Six

I visited the firm's ethics guru, Kevin Fox, when I returned to the office. I explained about the Barnard situation. He agreed that I had done the right thing.

"Perhaps," I said, "but Stanley was so angry, I was afraid that he might sue us for something."

"What could he possibly sue us for?"

"I have no idea," I said. "But don't disgruntled clients always sue their lawyers?"

"Not always," he said. "And of course it would help if you could ungruntle him."

"I'll do what I can," I said.

I left his office to go back to my own. Marion had another stack of pink telephone messages to hand to me. Since I had left BHC and its owners, I had accumulated several messages from Stanley and from Mrs. Barnard. I felt extremely uneasy.

I called Mrs. Barnard first.

"Jack," she said. "I just wanted to apologize for Stanley's behavior."

It made no sense to me that she would apologize for her son, who was an adult, at least nominally. Stanley was the one who had to apologize. But I deflected.

"I'm an adult, Mrs. Bernard," I said. "I've been in the business world long enough to roll with the punches."

"Well, just so you know," she said.

We made a few of the obligatory "good-bye" noises, and I hung up. Then I called Stanley.

"I want you to give me the name of a good trial lawyer," he said. No "hello."

"Okay," I said. "Let me get back to you with a few names."

"One name," he said. "One good lawyer." He hung up.

So much for apologies.

I sent out an email to all our lawyers, explaining that I was looking for a good litigator for a good client whom we could not represent. As I expected, within minutes I received five emails from the senior partners who served on the Firm Underwriting Committee, along the following lines: Are you sure we can't get waivers to represent the client in litigation? I then had to explain that it was litigation between the shareholders.

As I also expected, I received twelve emails suggesting good trial lawyers. Three of suggestions had the same name: Miles Sawyer. Miles was a so-called "conflicts" attorney, someone who stepped in when a firm had an ethical conflict and who never tried to poach a client from the referring law firm.

I sent Miles' name and contact information to Stanley via email.

I wasn't surprised to hear from Mrs. Barnard again the following week: her son had sued her, and she needed a lawyer. I repeated the procedure with her, and found another conflicts attorney, Vincent Phillips, to represent her. Since she was web-savvy, I emailed her Vinnie's information.

I thought then I would probably not hear another word from the BHC principals or the company for quite a while. But they dragged my ass into their craziness. And they weren't just a pain in the ass. They were a giant pain in the ass.

Chapter Seven

Larry Evans answered the knock at the door. It was his waiter, ready to remove his used plates. He stood back to let him in.

"Hey," said the waiter. "You ate that whole steak. Wow, I'm impressed. It was so bloody, it was practically uncooked. I see you haven't unpacked yet. Would you like one of our valets to unpack for you?"

Evans took a five dollar bill out of his pocket, and handed it to the waiter. He said nothing until the waiter, wheeling the room service table, was at the door. Then he said what he had to say.

"Shut up," he said. And he closed the door.

His cell rang. He checked the clock. Three p.m. eastern.

"What?" he said.

"Like the room?"

"It's fine."

"You are a taciturn man," his partner said.

"Get to the point."

"Well, Larry, my man, this job is going to be slow and steady. So there's no need to rush. We're getting paid by the day, with a bonus at the end."

"Who's the target?"

"Not over the phone."

Evans sighed. Cell phones could be tapped. Land lines could be tapped. Technology was a pain.

"We have a scenario for you."

Evans closed his eyes. He really hated all the background nonsense.

"Are you listening?"

"Yeah, go ahead," Evans said.

"You have to establish your background with the target."

Evans said nothing.

"Say 'uh-huh' every now and then so I know you're still there."

"Uh-huh," Evans said.

"I'll messenger over the background book."

"Uh-huh."

"I know you think these jobs are boring. But a little intellectual stimulation isn't going to kill you. And they're much more lucrative."

"Uh-huh."

"We'll set up a meeting when you've had a chance to review the material. Two days enough time?"

"Yes," Evans said. And he hung up the phone.

Goddamn cleverness was going to get them caught.

Chapter 8

I got an email from Vinnie. He and Miles wanted to set up a conference call to discuss "the Barnard situation." He put it in quotes. That can't be good.

I didn't want to do it. I like it better when I can put a period on the end of an episode and not have to think about it anymore. But according to Vinnie's email, both Mrs. Barnard and Stanley Barnard wanted me to explain the workings of the corporation to the lawyers. Both of them said that I was the corporation's lawyer. Lucky me.

As it turned out, we never had the conference call. Instead, I received a phone call from a police officer named Nathan Soloway. He was calling because a fistfight had erupted at BHC, and everyone wanted me to come and straighten things out.

"What?" I said.

"This is like a domestic disturbance, it seems to me," Officer Soloway said. "If you're willing to come down here to talk to everyone, it would be a hell of a lot better than if I have to arrest people."

"How many people are we talking about?" I said.

"Seems like four," he said.

"Four!"

"I know. Can you make it?"

"I'll be there in twenty minutes," I said.

"That's great. I appreciate it. And I'm sure your clients will, too."

Officer Soloway said that he would wait for my arrival, just in case my appearance didn't calm the waters.

It occurred to me that I should call Vinnie and Miles and let them know what was happening. They should be there, too. I called them both on my cell as I drove (hands-free, of course). Both said they would meet me at BHC.

We all converged on headquarters at the same time. There was one lone black and white police car, and a fire rescue truck. An EMT was leaning back on the truck, smoking a cigarette. Officer Soloway approached us.

"Officer," I said, and stuck out my hand. "These counsel represent the shareholders."

I quickly introduced Miles and Vinnie.

"What's going on?"

"Mr. Stanley Barnard appears to have struck his mother," Officer Soloway said.

Vinnie's jaw dropped. "What?"

"The EMTs told me that she's going to need a few stitches on her left cheek."

I shook my head.

"How could this happen?" I said. I knew it was a rhetorical question. Where human beings are involved, anything can happen.

"He struck his 93-year old mother?" Vinnie said.

"Punched her, according to her," said Officer Soloway. His face was unrevealing. Undoubtedly, he had seen elder abuse before, even among the rich.

Mrs. Barnard strode out of the office. She had a bandage on her cheek, with strips of tape holding it on her. A female EMT hurried after her, holding what seemed to be Mrs. Barnard's handbag.

Although she was headed toward the fire rescue truck, when she saw me and the knot of lawyers, she made a quick turn and walked toward us.

"Jack," she said. "You see what he did?"

I nodded.

"He's crazy, Jack," she said. She looked at the other lawyers, and at Nathan Soloway. Then she turned on her heel and walked to where the EMTs were standing, awaiting her presence. Officer Soloway followed her. Vinnie and Miles and I looked at each other, and headed for the office. At the last minute, Vinnie stopped.

"I should probably go with my client," he said, and ran toward the truck.

That left Miles and me. We continued our journey into the office. I was not looking forward to this. All I could think of was: maybe I should take that job where I don't have to have any clients. I made a mental note to call Catherine King when I got back to the office.

Chapter Nine

Larry Evans opened his suitcase. He would have to buy clothes. He expected to spend the cash on that. But he couldn't know what to buy until he knew more about who he was supposed to be.

He removed a black case with a lock. He reached into his pocket for the key. The lock opened on his first try. Inside, the steel gleaming, was a set of chef's knives. He kept them spotless. He didn't like to see crusted blood anywhere near the blade, and he kept the handles clean as well. He lifted a toiletry case out of the suitcase. In addition to a shaving kit, he had a small spray bottle of luminol. That helped him keep the knives bloodless.

He had a small package of latex gloves. He examined them for tears, and saw none.

The lining on the top of the suitcase had what looked like a small tear at the corner. He took a tweezers from his toiletry case and inserted it carefully into the lining. He drew out a thin but very strong piece of wire, loosely coiled. Each end of the wire had a small loop soldered in. He opened a small jewelry box in his toiletry set. It contained two identical bracelets, made of steel. Anyone noticing the bracelets might have seen that they were too small to fit his wrists. No one ever noticed.

He pulled out a small vial with three multicolored beetles, all dead. He returned it to his case. He opened a small compartment at the bottom of his suitcase, and removed a thirty-five caliber pistol. The ammunition rested in a pocket meant for shoes. Under the handle of the case, a hidden compartment contained a silencer for the weapon. His underwear and socks were strewn throughout the case, acting as cushioning for his tools.

He often used his head and his hands instead of his tools for his work, but he thought it wiser to have them with him, should the need arise. And it was good to have a choice. It was good to have options. Flexibility was the key. His own form of creativity.

He never carried with him any object he hadn't tested first. He remembered an old man he had met during the war, who had wounded himself badly using a makeshift garrote, a thin wire he had pulled from a junked car engine. The old man was intent on killing his target, and had pulled the ligature through the man's neck without regard to the pain it caused him. He had practically decapitated the victim. He accomplished his mission, but he severed all the tendons and ligaments in his hands. Larry Evans had no intention of letting that happen to him.

The steel bracelets worked as excellent handles for his garrote. He had tried it first on a mannequin, then on a dog. Perfect both times, and his hands were uninjured.

Generally, he had no particular feelings about any of his weapons, but looking at the garrote made him itch to try it again. He immediately thought of the annoying waiter. He suppressed the thought. He didn't need to complicate things.

He packed everything back into his suitcase, locked it, and placed it at the back of the closet. He awaited instructions. He knew one thing for sure:

they would not include losing the boots. He had made that clear. The boots were now a part of him. He'd had them for 25 years, and they were the most comfortable foot gear he'd ever had. There was a shoe repair store near his ranch that resoled and reheeled them every few years, while he sat waiting for them, barefoot, in a chair at the front of the shop. As soon as he left the service and his army boots behind, these boots had been his constant companions. If they needed someone to look like a businessman from Europe, he was not the guy to hire.

He sat in the armchair in his room, waiting. He was good at waiting.

Chapter Ten

Miles and I strode into the offices of Barnard Hardware as if we knew what we were doing. Various members of the office staff stood in small groups, whispering and wringing their hands. They looked up as we entered.

"Where's Mr. Barnard?" said Miles.

They all pointed silently, toward Mrs. Barnard's office. Miles and I glanced at each other before we made our way down the hall. In Mrs. Barnard's office, we found Stanley, sitting in one of his mother's guest chairs, looking morose and sucking on the knuckles of his right hand. When he removed them from his mouth, I could see bruising.

"What's going on?" I said. I sat on the edge of his mother's desk.

"She's crazy, Jack," he said.

"Who's crazier," I said, "a ninety-three year old assault victim or her son, the batterer?"

I was angry. I shouldn't have expressed myself so forcefully. Miles put on some spin for his client.

"She must have done something pretty horrendous," Miles said, "for you to be so mad you hit her."

"You have no idea," Stanley said. He looked grateful for Miles' understanding.

I wasn't buying it.

"You tell me, Stanley, what could possibly justify physical violence?"

"She tortures me," he said. He was mumbling, forcing me to lean in toward him. "She's relentless."

I inhaled the scent of alcohol. It was not medicinal alcohol. It had the tang of good scotch.

"Have you been drinking?" I said.

"None of your fucking business," he said.

"Now, now," said Miles.

"It is my fucking business, Stanley. You and your crazy family called us here."

"Well, now you can leave," he said.

Miles opened his mouth, but Stanley shut it for him.

"You too, you shyster," he said.

I didn't need to be asked twice, but I could see Miles hesitating. I grabbed his forearm and gently pulled him toward the door.

"Now is not the best time," I said.

"Get out!" Stanley said. Spittle formed at the corners of his mouth.

Several employees wandered slowly back toward us, to try to figure out what the noise was about.

"Nothing to see," I said.

Miles and I continued our walk toward the door.

"What the fuck?" said Miles. He was now walking forward without my gentle prodding.

"It's pointless to try to talk to him when he's drunk," I said.

"Yeah, but what's this with the attack on the old lady?"

"I have very little idea," I said. "Maybe your client will explain when he sobers up."

"If he sobers up," Miles said. He gave a quick wave and walked toward his car.

I thought Stanley was crazy. I was feeling sorry for Mrs. Barnard. And as for me, I was shocked, SHOCKED at what I had seen.

Clients, I thought. Can't live with them, can't live without them.

Chapter Eleven

Larry Evans was reading the background book his contact had sent. It was describing "Larry Evans," filling in details about his past and about what he was supposed to be doing in Philadelphia. He laughed out loud when he got to the part about appearing to be a kind and sympathetic listener. The date wasn't April 1, but this had to be a joke.

His room phone rang.

"What?" he said.

"Sorry, Mr. Evans," said a clerk. He sounded nervous. "Just trying to see if you want turndown service tonight."

"Never," he said, and slammed down the phone.

He continued reading. He wasn't dumb. He read a lot, particularly newspapers and news on the internet, and he realized that Larry Evans was supposed to be a Ted Turner/Michael Bloomberg kind of guy, steely and a good businessman but with a human side.

This might be one of the tougher jobs for him. He managed to pass as human when he was in public, but he didn't love the idea of appearing touchy-feely.

He was supposed to act as though he wanted to buy the victim's business. He was supposed to get close to the victim. And then he was supposed to remove the victim from the earth in whatever way he believed he could get away with. And then he was supposed to scram. Out of Philly as quickly as possible.

He finished reading the book, and then sat back. He had to flesh out the story line himself. He got up and checked himself in the bathroom mirror. He hated to shave his moustache, but he thought he had better do that. His hair was shaggy, and he thought that was fine. Later, when he was getting out of town, he'd shave his head. He knew from experience it would make him look entirely different. So far, in his entire professional career, no one had ever focused on his achilles' heel—his boots. Rarely did people focus on footwear, even the police when they sent out an all-points bulletin looking for him.

He nodded his head at himself in the mirror. He'd enjoy his moustache one more night. He'd do dinner at Morton's, eating another big steak, with a few glasses of good wine, and then see what he could find in the way of a quickie in a doorway. No point polluting the atmosphere of this fine hotel room when all he needed was a release.

He knew what he had to do. He was beginning to look forward to the enterprise. He put a "do not disturb" sign on his door handle, and headed out for his meal.

Chapter Twelve

As soon as I returned to my office, I called Catherine King. I wanted to shout: Get me out of here! But she wasn't in her office. I left a message for her to call me.

The head of our litigation department poked his head in.

"Hi, Donald," I said.

"I just had the most bizarre experience," he said.

"Me, too," I said.

"With the Firm Underwriting Committee?"

"No, with a client."

"Oh," he said. Then he sat down in one of my guest chairs.

Donald is a very nice man. Tall and handsome. Great teeth, still has all his hair. He is well-known among the lawyers in the firm for playing solitaire most of the day on his office computer.

"The FUC called me in to talk," Donald said. He pronounced it as we all did, "eff-you-see."

"I figured it was about the department, and I brought all of my information on budgets, billable hours, profitability…"

"I get it," I said, cutting him off.

"When I got there, it was Ron Kapinsky, and Will Karp. No one else."

Ron was chairman of the FUC. We all called him two-face, although not in front of him. He had what used to be called "wall-eyes." His eyes went in different directions. And Will Karp was a no-chinned gnome with an overbite. He wasn't on the Firm Underwriting Committee.

"Ron Kapinsky asked me what made me think I was the chairman of the department."

I stared at him. "What?"

"Apparently Will Karp wants to be chairman of the department."

"Don't the partners in the department get a vote?"

"That's how it's always been," Donald said.

"I seem to recall that's how you became chairman."

"Right," he said. "But that wasn't good enough, apparently. Because according to Ron, I was never the head of the department, so the FUC could put Will in as chairman."

I screwed up my eyes. "You've always been identified as the department chairman," I said. "Even on the firm's website."

Donald nodded. "I know that. You know that. But the FUC said it wasn't true, that I hadn't been appointed, and that Will was chairman."

"Wow. It's like waking up and finding out you're a cockroach."

Donald smiled weakly. "Yeah. Very kafka-esque."

"So what did you do?"

"I said 'you guys are crazy' and I dropped all my papers on the conference room table and left."

"What the heck is going on?" I said. I hated it when people messed with reality.

"I don't know," Donald said. "It's very disheartening."

"That's an understatement," I said. "It's actually more than that. It's downright scary. It's as if they told you your name isn't really Donald."

"Well, that's why I came to see you, Jack," he said. "I figured if you had the same reality I have, I'm not the one who's nuts."

"Unless we have a folie a deux," I said.

Donald snorted in a half-hearted way.

Two-face walked into my doorway.

"Donald," he said, "I wanted to talk to you about the department's profitability. Could you come down to talk to the FUC?"

Donald looked glazed. I realized my heart was pounding.

"Is he the head of the department again?" I said.

"I don't know what you mean," Two-face said. "Will Karp is the head of the department."

"Since when?" I said.

"Always," Two-face said.

"They're gaslighting you, Donald," I said.

"Are you casting aspersions on me? On the FUC?" Two-face said.

"Absolutely," I said. "I've never heard anything so wicked in my life."

Two-face turned one of his two eyes on me. "Just because you're retiring doesn't mean you can make trouble around here."

"If telling the truth is making trouble, than brand me a trouble-maker," I said.

Later, I would wonder if this had been the most tactful thing to say to a vindictive liar.

Chapter 13

Larry Evans wiped his mouth and his moustache with satisfaction. He had eaten an enormous steak, bloody rare, as he sat on a banquette watching the other diners. Morton's always delivered. He had drunk most of a bottle of a California merlot blend that he enjoyed. He contemplated ordering dessert.

He could read certain people very well, usually those who were most like him. The waiter and he had exchanged a look at the beginning of the meal, and he knew the man had interests other than serving great food at an expensive restaurant. Undoubtedly the waiter could offer him entertainment running the gamut from girls to boys to drugs. A useful new buddy.

When the waiter brought over the dessert menu, he and Larry had a cryptic conversation that both understood well. Larry now knew where to go after his fine meal. He tipped the waiter the customary twenty two percent, and left him a hundred dollar bill under his plate.

He walked back to his hotel in order to let his meal settle in. Not far, but enough to start the digestive juices. He went back to his room, took a piss. He opened his suitcase, and stared at its contents. He shook his head, and closed it again. He put it into the closet. He left his room.

His good buddy had suggested he might enjoy a stroll on Camac street. He walked down Walnut Street toward the Delaware River, peering down each cross street until he found Camac. It was a tiny street, really no more than an alley. It ran past a theater, and then past bars and even a few restaurants. The street lights didn't illuminate too much, which was fine with him.

He knew he had strolled to the right area when voices started coming at him from the darker parts of the street. "Hey, Sugar," they said. Or "Hey, handsome," or even cruder, "want to do me?" He felt himself get hard as the voices crowded in. A tall brunette in ridiculous high heels and a very short skirt grabbed his belt buckle.

"You're ready for me, aren't you big guy?" she whispered.

He pushed her into a doorway and unzipped his pants. He handed her a hundred dollar bill, which was the smallest he had on him. She tucked it into her small handbag, and knelt down on the bag to do her thing on her knees. When she was finished, he grabbed her hair with his left hand while his heartbeat returned to normal.

"Hey," she said, as he pulled her hair. The voice sounded masculine. Not that he cared. "Rough stuff costs extra."

He didn't know why, but that made him mad. It came over him like a seizure. He bent slightly at the knees, closer to her level on the street on her knees, and put his right hand around her throat. She/he tried to rise off the ground, but her position put her at a disadvantage, and he kept up the pressure on her throat until he could get his thumb onto one carotid and his third finger on the other. She/he passed out quickly, and he kept up the pressure. When he was certain she was dead, he placed her carefully back in the doorway, in the shadows. Probably she wouldn't be found for a while, possibly not until the morning.

He was glad his DNA wasn't on file anywhere. He headed back up Camac and took the first cross street back to Broad Street. He sauntered back to his hotel. At no time did he hear shouts from Camac. Nor did he hear sirens. He smiled.

He entered the hotel, and took the elevator to his room. He shrugged out of his clothes after removing his boots. He headed for the bathroom, and fixed himself a nice hot shower. He shampooed his long hair, and even, for fun, his moustache. In the morning he would shave it.

He went to bed immediately, sliding in between the cool clean sheets in his bare skin. He fell into a dreamless sleep. It had been a perfect evening.

Chapter 14

The rumors started that very afternoon. According to them, I was losing interest in the well-being of the firm. There was concern that I was bad-mouthing the firm to clients. I was no longer a team player. And on and on.

At first, the lawyers at the firm met the rumors with sarcasm and disbelief. Several of my friends assured me that they didn't believe any of it.

"Hey, Jack," a friend said. "Who did you piss off?"

We laughed. Oh, how we laughed.

However, there is a difference between the truth and the narrative that people create to make themselves feel better. I know about the narrative. By the end of my tenure at the firm, the rumors had become received wisdom. In other words, I truly had tried to destroy the firm. So, good riddance to me.

Of course, I had my own feelings of relief when I left. The games of the workplace had ceased to intrigue me. In fact, they were exhausting. Not surprising that I found a new world to enter and discover. I never thought that the Barnards' problems would help me find a solution to my own. But they did.

Chapter 15

Larry Evans awakened without the aid of a wake-up call. He felt as though he was bursting with energy. He practically threw himself out of bed and into the shower, where he took his razor and shaving cream. Off with the facial hair! He almost enjoyed removing it. He always enjoyed starting a new project. Even if it meant losing his stache.

He cleaned up his shaving job at the bathroom mirror. He stared at himself. Not bad looking, he supposed. He looked into his own eyes. He didn't see anything there except a dark iris. He crinkled the skin around his eyes slightly, a trick he had practiced to look amused and warm.

"There I go," he said. "Warm interested businessman with lots of heart."

He tried the phrase over again, and then said "Larry Evans" a few times. He decided to emphasize his country twang a bit for the folks he was meeting.

He dressed in jeans, a blue collared shirt and a leather suit jacket, and put on a bolo tie for the finishing touch. And of course, his boots.

He checked to be sure that the "do not disturb" sign was still on the door handle of the room. He looked at his watch. Eight a.m. Too early to make his business call. Perfect timing for some breakfast.

He remembered seeing a diner on the corner opposite his hotel. Not a great suburban diner, with a giant footprint and a menu the size of a book. Not an out-in-the-country diner, made from an old railroad car, or a shack, with lots of weak hot coffee and a menu that never changed. This was a city diner, with fake old neon signs and youthful, well-dressed diners. The diner was the first floor of an office building. He expected the coffee would be strong, the way he liked it, and the omelets filled with unusual ingredients, to give his gourmet side some enjoyment.

He walked to the diner, inhaling the cool damp air with its hint of diesel fumes. He wasn't disappointed when he entered and sat at the counter. It was just as he had expected. He ordered a large coffee and a swiss cheese, kale and caramelized onion omelet. He allowed the counter person to talk him into some quinoa bread, toasted. When his meal arrived, he stared into space and concentrated on it, savoring the tastes. It was a beautiful breakfast.

He felt terrific. What a great day to meet new people.

Chapter 16

"Hey Dad, how's life?"

It was my daughter Monica on the phone. Monica, too, was a lawyer. Unlike her old dad, making pots of money in a law firm, she was a lawyer for the Environmental Protection Agency. She was passionate about protecting the environment. She didn't mind the low pay and long hours. Ah, to be young, and have a rich father.

"The usual horrible office politics and wretched clients," I said. I never kept anything from Monica. She was an intelligent woman who had much the same understanding of human frailty as my late wife, her mother. I could talk to her about anything.

"What's new with you?"

"I have a new case," she said. "And I'd like to brainstorm it with you."

My ego expanded.

"Want to do lunch?" I said.

"Let me cook dinner for you, Dad," she said. "Tonight okay?"

Monica was too kind to say what she knew— her old dad didn't go out much anymore.

"Sure, that would be great," I said.

"Great, seven at my place," she said.

"See you then," I said.

It cheered me to think of seeing her. She has always been a delightful person, both as a child and as an adult. It helps to have a good person to connect with. My late wife was like that, too. Sometimes I really missed her. Ironically, it was often when I was with Monica, the light of my life, that I missed her mother the most.

The phone rang again. It was Catherine King.

"So now you've seen the wisdom of my offer," she said. She didn't even say hello first.

"Let's say I'm considering it more carefully now," I said.

"I'll see what I can set up. What's your availability for this week?"

I consulted my calendar and gave her some free time slots. When I hung up, I was strangely unelated. What was the point of exchanging one stressful situation for another? I mulled this over for awhile. My phone rang again. This time, it was Mrs. Barnard.

"Jack," she said, "Stanley's in the hospital."

The family saga continued. I realized that I would like it to continue without me.

"I'm very sorry," I said, "I hope he recovers quickly."

"My son is an idiot," she said. "He took one of those erectile dysfunction pills, and he's taking heart medicine. Bad interaction."

Many questions crowded into my head. What doctor would have prescribed such pills for a man with a heart condition? What woman would have wanted him to take such medication? Was he cheating on his wife now?

But all I said was: "Gee, Mrs. Barnard. I'm so sorry."

"Please Jack," she said. "Go visit him. Talk to him. You were always able to talk sense into him. He's killing himself. At this rate, I'll outlive him.

Although, I'm not sure that would be such a bad thing for the business."

I tried to beg off, but she was adamant. I finally promised to see him in a few hours, just to get her off the phone without being rude. Her persistence was annoying, but I knew that was how she had built her business. Never take no for an answer.

I decided that my best course of action was to get over to the hospital, let Stanley berate me for a while, and then go to Monica's for dinner. That way, I could get through the hideous part of the day with thoughts of the later pleasant part of the day to take the edge off.

But first, paperwork. A young lawyer had prepared a brief to be filed next week for one of my clients, and I wanted to read it and edit it as quickly as possible. I took off my jacket, hung it behind my door, and closed the door. I was ready to buckle down and do some billable work.

As I sat down, I heard a knock at my door. I sighed. Office politics, undoubtedly, and it just might push me over the edge today. I decided to act as though I was too absorbed in what I was doing to acknowledge the knock. Maybe whoever it was would go away.

The door opened. It was Eldon Soloway, one of my law partners.

"Hey, hey Jack," he said, heading directly for my chair. "I thought maybe you couldn't hear my knock."

I stared at him as he settled himself. Eldon often looked unkempt, and today was no exception.

His shirttail was unhinged from his pants at the back, and his thinning hair was standing up in tufts, as though he'd been running his hands through it.

"Have you heard the latest?" he said.

"No," I said. "And I have a brief I have to work on."

"Sure, sure," Eldon said. "But I know you never leave anything to the last minute."

"What's up, Eldon," I said. I leaned back in my chair. I guessed this would take a while.

"H-h-have you heard about Donald? He became a non-person."

Eldon had a stutter when he was excited. He was also able to use it at will to his advantage. I'd seen him once make an opening statement to a jury where his stuttering was calibrated to ensure that all eyes were on him, and him alone, as he spoke. "L-l-l-ladies and j-j-j-j-j..." he said. The jurors leaned forward in their seats, worrying that he couldn't get the words out, and then, once he had them trained to watch him, he lost the stutter.

"Well, I heard that Donald was told he never was the head of the department. Is that what you mean?"

Eldon cackled.

"B-b-better than that," he said. "Now the Exec is telling him that the partnership agreement never legally made him a partner."

"What?" I could almost not believe it. But, of course, I could.

"I don't really know the thinking," he said. "Do you?"

"Honestly, Eldon, I'm clueless," I said. "We may want to rethink the makeup of our Firm Underwriting Committee. Maybe have a recall election."

"They'll probably tell us we don't actually have a right under the partnership agreement to elect the FUC," Eldon said.

I felt myself getting agitated.

"I think those idiots are subjecting our firm to a lawsuit, Eldon."

He nodded his head.

"You're probably right."

"And that's a good reason to un-elect them," I said.

Eldon looked at his watch.

"Whoa, gotta go," he said.

He leaped out of his chair. He left my office, waving his hand.

And I sat, staring at the empty seat, remembering that Eldon was a gossip, and most likely could be counted on to repeat my remarks to the FUC. I was beginning to feel as though I was working in a police state where one's children could be spying for the secret police.

I shook off the thought, and concentrated on the brief I was supposed to be reading. I read it, and began to feel a sense of wonder. This was actually a great brief! Well written, clear, persuasive…and no typos. How profoundly satisfying.

I emailed a quick note to my associate, praising the brief, and signing off on it. Then I threw the brief into the trash and put on my suit jacket. I needed to get out of the office. A visit to Stanley in the hospital wasn't going to cheer me up, but at least I'd be out of this hotbed of insanity.

I decided to walk to the hospital, one of the earliest medical establishments in our country's history. My walk took me from the small canyon that is downtown Philadelphia to the leafy streets of historic houses in Society Hill. It was a beautiful day, and the sun and warm air almost made me forget why I was out of the office.

I paused as I passed the gated lawn and garden, ablaze with many colors of azaleas. I remembered when Monica was born at this hospital; the garden echoed my joy at her arrival. And then I remembered when my wife died at this hospital. Then the garden had mocked me with its beauty.

I walked toward the visitor entrance. Visiting Stanley Barnard was going to be neither joyous nor devastating for me. But on a scale of one to ten…well, you get the idea.

Chapter 17

Larry Evans took a yellow cab from his hotel to the address he'd been given in his instructions. The cab driver told him the address was close to the Delaware River. Evans asked the driver to let him off a few blocks away; he liked walking around water.

As he exited the cab, he looked around, interested that the waterfront looked so scummy here. He paid the driver, and walked slowly down the street toward the water. He could smell the aroma of river water, with a tang of spilled oil and a hint of rotting garbage. To his right, he saw a massive complex with a fence surrounding it. The sign on the gate said: Barnard Hardware Company. Street lights on poles, outfitted with solar panels, dotted the street at regular intervals. On his left, the source of the garbage smell came into view: a huge hangar, roofed but open on three sides, with piles of garbage sitting and stewing in the morning sun.

Larry Evans was not squeamish, but the ripe smell was so intense it brought up an involuntary spasm in his diaphragm. He stopped walking and took a deep breath through his mouth. He sincerely hoped he was not going to have to hang around the area for too many days, and that the offices were not infected with the smell.

Once he got his gut under control, he continued walking toward the river. He was beginning to acclimate to the constant smell. He supposed that's how people who worked around the area could stand it. He stood at the water's edge, taking in the rotting piers, the weeded river bank and the garbage floating among the reeds, caught by the strands of grass and weeds. Across the river, he saw a raft of barges and tugs tied from piers at the water's edge into the river. He stood in his spot and turned around in a circle, seeing what there was to see. Much to his surprise, there were small clapboard houses visible just beyond the trash pile, neatly kept and obviously occupied. Over all, he preferred his little piece of heaven in the fields to this fetid mess. But he certainly had to take into account the presence of potential witnesses.

He turned away from the river, and began to walk back toward his target. His blood was pumping in his ears. He loved the beginning of a job.

Chapter 18

Stanley Barnard was sitting up in his hospital bed, surrounded by monitors, looking alive and surprisingly well. He was spluttering at the nurse beside him, who seemed about to take his blood pressure.

"Goddamn it," he said. "You just took that cuff off me."

"That's because your pressure is stabilized," said the nurse, "so we don't have to keep one on you all the time."

"Then why are you taking my goddamn blood pressure?" he said.

Stanley caught sight of me. He rolled his eyes.

"Do what you have to do," he said.

The nurse quickly measured his blood pressure with the hand-held cuff and a stethoscope. She nodded.

"Still good," she said.

"Even after my little tantrum?" Stanley said.

"Even after," the nurse said.

She turned to leave. She winked at me.

"You seem to be good as new," I said. "Or maybe better."

Stanley groaned.

"Listen, Jack, I'm royally pissed off about being in here. My body is not cooperating with my inner man."

I didn't say what I was thinking, which was "lose weight or shut up," or even "stop cheating on your wife or shut your pie hole."

"What does your inner man want, Stanley?" I said.

He looked at me as I stood beside his bed, his fleshy eyelids hooding his bloodshot eyes.

"I want to be able to eat as much as I want, I want to drink as much as I want, I want to fuck till my pecker falls off, and I want my mother to die."

What a great guy, I thought. Not.

"How about being as handsome as Warren Beatty in his prime?" I said.

"Heh, heh, heh," he said. "I never was much for the looks, Jack. The ladies love me for the money."

I tried to peek at my wristwatch. I'd only been here a few minutes, but it felt like days. Stanley saw the movement.

"Hey, Jack, you don't have to hang around. I'll prolly be out tomorrow. I appreciate the visit."

I felt embarrassment creep up my face as a red, hot flush.

"Sorry, Stanley," I said. "I have an appointment with my daughter. I'm anxious to see her."

"Go, Jack. I'll let you know if I need anything."

I tried back-pedaling about leaving, but Stanley shooed me away. He asked me to hand him the newspaper that was sitting on a visitor chair on my way out. I did as he asked, and then waved at him on my way out. He didn't notice; he was already reading the paper.

I held my breath until I got into the elevator, then I exhaled. Really couldn't wait now to see Monica. I was very curious to see what she wanted to discuss with me. I decided to buy a bottle of wine at the state store on my way back to the office.

There was a crowd near the store, and beyond the crowd I could see yellow police tape cordoning off an alley. As I entered the state store, I noticed that the clerks, the manager, and most of the customers were standing at the plate glass window, trying to get a view of the action.

"What's going on?" I said to the manager.

"They found a body, I think," she said.

"Wow," I said.

"I know, not very surprising around here. The cops think it's a working girl."

"A prostitute," I said.

"That makes her sound too high class," said one of the customers. "She was a skank."

I gave him an icy glare, but it was wasted on him, since he was still peering out the window.

"I hate that word," the manager said.

"Me, too," I said.

I wandered over toward the California reds. Monica and I shared a taste for fruity varietals. The Pennsylvania state liquor store system didn't usually yield outstanding results for wine, but I found a small vineyard bottle of pinot noir that would work fine, and took it to the register. All the employees were still looking out the window.

"Excuse me," I said.

The manager turned and caught my eye. She nodded, and came behind the counter.

"I hate that the girls who work around here are expendable," she said.

She rang up my purchase, and handed the bottle to me in a paper bag.

"What's the likelihood that someone will get charged for that poor girl's murder?" she said.

"How do you know it wasn't a drug overdose?" I said.

She sighed.

"I don't know. But you know what? That's murder too, in my book."

I nodded sagely. Then I held up the bag of wine.

"Thank you," I said.

"Sure," she said.

I walked out of the store, passing again the crowd of gawkers. I hate to admit it, but by the time I walked into the next block, I'd already forgotten about the tumult. My mind had reverted to thoughts of dinner with my daughter. How great was that going to be? She was living in a quaint trinity on a small cobbled street just off Pine Street, and she had furnished it so that it was comfortable and cheerful. I always felt good when I visited her there.

What I didn't know at the time was that Monica's life would soon be in danger, and that an unlikely ally would help me save her.

Chapter 19

Larry Evans walked toward the pile of garbage, looking for the office he had been told to head for. There it was, a small yellow brick building, nestled in near the pile, with a large red sign reading "TMI Waste Transfer Station." The closer he got to the building, the more aromatic the pile was, until he felt as though his head was full of the smell and that it would explode.

But as soon as he walked into the building, through two glass doors, the smell vanished. He was in air-conditioned, air-filtered comfort. He felt his head deflating, like a balloon that had come untied.

A tall, skinny man with a shock of red hair, spiking up on his head, stood up from a desk he'd been sitting on when Evans walked in.

"Hey," he said. "I'm Rick Kozak. You must be Larry Evans."

Evans put out his hand.

"I guess you don't get that many visitors here, am I right?"

Kozak laughed.

"The smell is pretty overpowering," he said.

The men shook hands.

"I believe that's an understatement," Evans said.

"Come on in," Rick said. "The family's waiting for you in the conference room."

Rick lead the way down a small corridor. The hall had doors on either side. Rick pointed to one on the left. It had a hand-lettered sign that said

"Conference Room." He held up a hand in front of Evans.

"Don't get too upset at whatever Old Rick says," Rick said. "What's important is what everyone else thinks."

"Okay," said Evans.

Rick opened the door. There were four people at a conference table, three of whom turned toward the door when it opened. The fourth scowled down at the table, as if something there infuriated him. Larry Evans figured this was "Old Rick."

"Hi folks," said Rick. "This is Larry Evans."

There were two women and a man who raised their hands and said "Hi, Larry." Old Rick looked up from the table, his rheumy eyes blazing with hatred.

"Fuck you, Larry," Old Rick said.

"Oh, for pity's sake, Rick. Don't be like that," said the older woman.

"Fuck you, too, Gladys," Old Rick said.

Larry Evans put out his right hand toward the woman named Gladys.

"Glad to be in such good company, ma'am," he said.

Everyone laughed, even Old Rick. Doing what I'm supposed to, Larry Evans thought. Being charming.

Old Rick was the big kahuna here, and he motioned Larry to a chair. Then he began to speak. His voice was like fresh whole walnuts rolling down a gravel hill.

"My family wants to sell our business. Our family has run this business for almost a hundred years. It's always provided a good living. So why should we?"

Larry Evans allowed his face to show surprise.

"Almost a century. That's something," he said.

"We grew up with the stink," Old Rick said. "And you know what my father told me if I made a face, or I complained? That's the smell of money."

"Everyone needs a place to put their garbage," said Rick.

"It's as reliable as death and taxes," said Old Rick.

"Except that now there are environmental safeguards in place that cost money," said Gladys.

"And now we have to clean up whatever mess our family made in the past," said Rick. "Which is where you come in."

Larry Evans nodded. He played the investor.

"How much cleanup are you expecting? Have you estimated the cost?"

Old Rick snorted.

"If you're asking us those questions, I already know that any deal you offer to make with us is going to be too little. You might as well leave now."

"Daddy," said Gladys.

"Well, now," said Evans.

And then he stopped. He wasn't stupid, but he didn't know a tremendous amount about Pennsylvania environmental laws, and he didn't feel as though he could stray too far from the information in the book. He reviewed in his mind the scenario he was supposed to float.

"Money isn't the only way to get a deal done," he said.

"Fuck that," said Old Rick.

"If you wanted to take some of the cleanup off our hands, that's as good as money," said Gladys.

Old Rick glared at her.

"You short-sighted babies. Don't you know that if we don't sell, we don't have to do any cleanup? We can just keep going on how we've been going on."

"But Daddy," Gladys said, "what if none of us wants to run the business?"

Old Rick opened his mouth, and then closed it. He shook his head.

Larry Evans was glad that he wasn't really here to invest in or buy the family's business. Old Rick was tough as nails, and he clearly wasn't going to give his consent to a change in ownership. And as Larry knew from his briefing book, Old Rick owned 51% of the stock.

Evans' real reason for being here would play out over the next few days. For now, he smiled and smiled, and looked concerned, and nodded his head, whatever was appropriate to each point the family made in their debate. Mr. Charm.

Chapter 20

Monica took the wine bottle from me with real pleasure. I gave her a brief hug and kiss, and could smell a hint of the peachy scent of her shampoo.

"We're having veal, Dad, so this is perfect," she said.

"I'll try to pretend I was able to read your mind," I said.

"Like you did when I was little?"

Monica laughed, and motioned for me to join her in the kitchen.

Her mother and I had her convinced when she was a girl that we knew her every movement and activity, even when she was out of our sight. She didn't realize then that parents, being adults with more years of experience, could make reasonable deductions based on evidence.

Like the time we let her stay by herself at home while we went out to dinner, and came home to find the cat playing with the cap from a bottle of beer. I didn't say anything to her that night, but the next day, I asked her how she liked the beer she drank. Her eyes had widened in surprise.

Or the time when she was even younger, and her mother had forbade her to walk in or run in or even get near the street. A neighbor walked by later, as my wife and daughter were weeding the garden. "Oh, hello," the neighbor said. "You're the little girl I saw playing in the street this morning." For years after that, Monica was sure we both had a network of eyes and ears watching her every move.

"Parents always know everything," I said as she handed me a corkscrew.

"I know," Monica said. "That's why I wanted to talk to you about this environmental issue."

She lifted the lid off a dutch oven, and the aroma of tomatoes, garlic and onions filled the air. I suddenly realized that I was starved.

"How soon to dinner?" I said.

"Right now," she said.

She ladled large portions of the veal stew into big bowls. I could see potatoes, pearl onions, carrots and pale chunks of veal. If I hadn't been so well-mannered, I'd be slavering onto my shirt.

As so often happens with wonderful meals, we eaters were mostly quiet as we happily ate everything Monica had cooked, which required several bowls full of stew. Our talk was small talk, with punctuation by "ummms" and "yums" throughout. When we finished, we finally sat back, and began to really talk.

I told Monica about the dysfunction at the law firm. She told me, not without a certain satisfaction at her superior position, that she loved working for the government, or as she said, the "good guys."

Then she got down to her questions.

"Dad, you know the transfer station down by the river, near Barnard Hardware?"

"Of course," I said. "My nose knows it well."

"That's what I wanted to ask your advice about."

I raised my eyebrows.

"Right now, the ground under the transfer station is polluted," she said.

I nodded my head.

"Probably, some of the pollution is making it into the Delaware River," she said.

"Delightful," I said. "Garbage juice in the river."

"But because the property is in a state Enterprise Zone and is in a Special Industrial Area as designated by Pennsylvania, it's unlikely that anyone will have to deal with it."

"What's all that mean?" I said.

Monica laughed.

"There are two different answers. As an EPA lawyer, my explanation is that it's a free pass for buyers of industrial property who don't want to clean up the contamination. A Pennsylvania lawmaker would say that it encourages businesses to reuse old industrial sites."

I raised an eyebrow.

"The Pennsylvania law says that if you buy a polluted industrial site, and it's in an enterprise zone, you have to study it, but you don't have to clean it up unless someone's life is at stake from the pollution."

"I don't get it," I said. "You work for the feds. When I was in law school, they taught us that federal law always trumped state laws."

"Now dad," she said. "You know that's too simplistic. Federal environmental law allows the federal government to delegate regulation and cleanup of wastes to the state."

"Even if you don't think the state's doing a good job?"

"Well, you just put the bunny into the hat," she said. "The EPA has to determine whether the state program is good enough to substitute for federal oversight."

"Oh, and someone already decided that the Commonwealth of Pennsylvania's environmental oversight is a good federal substitute."

"Right."

"This is fascinating, sweetheart," I said. "But you didn't want to debate federalism or politics with me, did you?"

"We have done that before, you know."

"When you were a passionate law student, we did."

Monica laughed.

"No, Dad, I actually want to talk to you about something more tangible."

"Are you thinking of investing in the transfer station?"

Monica's laugh disappeared.

"No, but someone else is," she said.

I nodded.

"And if the owners sell, there's very little likelihood that the new owners will do any cleanup."

"Continued trash juice in the river," I said.

She nodded.

"Exactly."

"So what kind of advice can I give you?"

"I'd just like to talk it through with you," she said. "Maybe I can use some moral suasion with someone, even if I can't enforce any cleanup."

"In my experience with the government," I said, "using a carrot instead of a stick is very rare."

"I'm sort of desperate, Dad. I feel strongly about this."

So while she plied me with homemade chocolate brownies, which she promised had no hallucinogens in them, we gabbed and role-played for the next two hours. At the end of it all, I wasn't sure how much, or even if, I had helped her. But she seemed to have come to a decision of some kind as I prepared to leave.

"Dad, you've really helped me," she said, kissing my cheek. "I think I know what to do. Thanks."

As I left, I reflected on how committed she was to her cause. Imagine trying to persuade instead of using the long arm of the law! What a rare and wonderful daughter I had.

Neither of us could see, however, that she was setting herself on a course for disaster.

Chapter 21

Larry Evans was wiped out by the time he left the transfer station. It wasn't just playing a role that was tiring, although it was. He much preferred just being himself, figuring out a way to eliminate whoever he was supposed to eliminate, and then going home to his farm.

No, it was more than the role-playing. It was trying to cope with a small roomful of monsters and harridans without losing his cowboy charm. Old Rick was hateful, even to Larry, who didn't either love or hate anyone. He spewed venom upon his family, and eventually upon Larry, at the end of the meeting, calling into question the legitimacy of their births, the race of their ancestors (with a clear preference for the white race), and their intellectual abilities. The capper for Larry was Old Rick telling young Rick that he was a bastard whose mother had whored herself with a gorilla and that young Rick's stupidity was a result of her sin. The fact that some family members had buried their heads in their hands hadn't alleviated his disgust for the whole group.

The worst part was that he had to do it again tomorrow. This time, Old Rick told him to come at 5 p.m. to join him for a drink. Then the family would reconvene at 6. Evans was tempted to walk out the door and never return, and he was also tempted to take his gun to the meeting and simply eliminate all of them. But he knew he would do neither. For some reason, his employer wanted him to play out the scenario of the interested buyer before he made his move. And he always followed orders. Unless, of course, it was impossible for some reason.

But he would never let anger be his guiding principle. Anger undermined what he did so well. He briefly thought of the prostitute he had killed, and mentally berated himself for the act. He had allowed anger to guide his hand, and it could have resulted in his arrest. He was determined not to allow it to happen again. He had to be cool. Always.

Back at his hotel, he saw he had a message on the hotel phone. It was his contact, looking for an update. He told Larry he would call back in an hour. The message had been an hour ago. And like clockwork, the phone rang.

"What," said Larry.

"Everything okay?" his partner said.

"Of course," Larry said.

"I have a long list of new jobs for you. Let's get this one over with."

"Nothing would make me happier," he said. "You're the one who's slowing me down."

"Not me, buddy. It's our client."

"It seems as though it's just a few more days. At least according to the play book."

"And then I have a nice new job in a beautiful island paradise."

"I'll take the island," Larry said. "I might need a vacation after this one."

His partner laughed.

"You never take a vacation," he said. "You getting old?"

Larry said nothing.

"Hey, buddy, just joking," his partner said. He knew Larry's capabilities.

"I got that," Larry said. Then he hung up.

He would go back to the steakhouse for dinner. Got to keep his strength up. And no more extracurricular activities. He needed to keep his wits about him.

He walked over to the restaurant. He was pleased they had a table for him, in the bar. The bar was quieter at this time of day. And there was less chance of running into his new friend, the waiter. He wanted to avoid any questions about his activities the night of the prostitute murder.

"Hi," said a female waiter. "I'm Brandy."

"Hi, Brandy," said Larry. "Unsweetened iced tea for me, please."

Brandy looked disappointed. She probably thought big tippers didn't drink iced tea.

He looked over the menu, and decided to order the biggest steak. It wasn't his money that would pay for it. But it would net Brandy a bigger tip.

She brought the tea, and he ordered. She smiled broadly, and left him to his tea.

He sipped it. Suddenly, he was overwhelmed. It was peach tea. It was a taste he remembered from early childhood, when his mother made it for him on the hottest days. It was a flavor he avoided like the plague. He didn't want the memory. He thought he wouldn't have to ask in a steakhouse whether or not the tea was flavored.

He sat still at his table. He found he was gulping, and breathing carefully. He tried to keep his breathing even. He needed to keep it even. By the time Brandy returned to the table, expressing concern, he had pulled himself back from the past.

"Sorry, sir, you don't like the tea?" Brandy said.

"Not into flavored teas," he said. "Make it a beer instead. Whatever local beer you have on tap."

"Absolutely," Brandy said. "I'm sorry, I should have asked…"

Larry raised a hand.

"It's fine, Brandy. Thanks."

He refused to think. He had to consciously keep his hands away from his face. Because all he wanted to do was put his head in his hands and cry.

But he didn't.

Chapter 22

Mrs. Barnard surprised me by appearing, without notice, at my office door.

"Mrs. Barnard," I said. "I wasn't expecting you."

I rose to usher her to a chair. She had a bandage on her face, but otherwise appeared unscathed. At close range, I could see the fine lines around her eyes, and the shiny spots on her cheeks that gave away her secret facelift. The liver spots on her hands certainly gave away her age. The combination of her pale, unrealistically smooth cheeks and her odd wig-hair gave her the look of a store mannequin.

"I'm fine, Jack, no need to hover," she said. "Just a few stitches."

As if she had read my mind, she added: "Not for the first time, of course."

She waved me away and took one of my visitor chairs.

"This isn't a social call," she said.

She smiled as if to soften the words, but it didn't reach to her eyes. Her eyes were watchful behind her glasses.

"You know," I said, "that I'm conflicted out of taking your side or your son's."

"I know," she said. "This has to do with our property. I received this in the mail."

She handed over a sheet of paper with the letterhead of a well-known local environmental consultant, Bill Cullen.

"What's this?" I said. "You know I'm not familiar with environmental issues."

She smiled at me again, this time broadly enough so I could see the edges of her false teeth.

"But your daughter is," she said.

"Monica? Monica works for the government. If you're having any problems on your property, you need to hire a private lawyer."

"This wouldn't be hiring, exactly."

I stared at her.

"What would this be, exactly?"

"I see this as you helping me to become educated about the environmental issues. By talking to your daughter."

I glanced at the letter she had handed to me. It was not about the Barnard property. It was about the property across the street from it, the malodorous transfer station. The last paragraph caught my attention. My daughter's name leapt out at me. Bill Cullen, the consultant, explained that the environmental issues on the property were being handled at the federal level by Monica.

"Jack, I need your help here," she said.

"It makes no sense for you to hire me to do environmental work. That's not what I do."

I was feverishly running through attorney conflict of interest rules in my head to determine if I could even take on such a representation.

"I know that," she said. "It would be a favor. I'm not hiring you. I want you to find out what the government is thinking about the property."

"Why don't you hire a lawyer to approach the EPA? Why don't you call yourself?"

"I don't want their public response. I want to know what they really want."

"I can't ask my daughter to divulge her client's confidential position," I said.

This, I knew, would be unethical.

"I don't understand that," she said. "You're a lawyer. She's a lawyer."

"It's unethical," I said.

"Why?"

"Lawyers are supposed to maintain their client's confidences."

"But you're family," she said. "She'd be helping you with a client."

I closed my eyes. It was ironic that the property was the one Monica had spoken to me about at dinner. And I was telling my client that I couldn't ask Monica to divulge the government's confidential position. I remembered an old radio show where the tag line was: "What a revoltin' development this is."

Was I being too rigid about the ethical considerations?

"I've been told on good authority," she said, "that your daughter is being very unyielding when it comes to discussing the cleanup of the property. I think you can make her see reason."

"Mrs. Barnard," I said, "I might be able to tell my daughter she is being unreasonable if you were to hire me as your lawyer and I were to take the case. But I can't do it behind the scenes as her father."

"Then I'll hire you," she said.

I shut my eyes. I made a wish, that she would disappear. When I opened them, she was still there.

"I can't take the case, Mrs. Barnard," I said. "I'm sorry."

"I think you're being very stubborn and unreasonable about this, Jack."

The headline in my head screamed: Pot Calls Kettle Black!

"That may be," I said. "But I still can't take the case."

"How about if I hire you as a lobbyist?" she said. "Then it's clear you're advocating for a position."

I patiently explained that in our state, a lobbyist had to be registered as a lobbyist. I was not.

We went around like this several more times, and when I heard her sigh, I knew that she would soon depart. I was correct. She also refused to shake my hand goodbye, waving me away like a fly.

I thought the Barnards were finally done with me. I knew for sure that, although I had no real reason to "fire" them as clients (after all, they paid their bills on time), I was becoming really sick to death of both of them. I might have to fire them for my own peace of mind. Or maybe the hand of fate would intervene, and both Barnards, one very old and the other very debilitated, would pass to the great beyond, and I would be done with them.

Really, I should have known to be careful what I wished for.

Chapter 23

The man currently known as Larry Evans made his way to the transfer station using public transportation. He had the time, and it was always a good idea to scope out escape routes. Routes, plural. Just as he liked to have options in the way he accomplished his assignments. No point in succeeding at them only to be caught getting away.

He remembered reading about a failed bank robbery in New York City, and he had absorbed the lessons embedded in that fiasco. Three men had robbed a bank during a busy lunch hour. They hadn't figured out contingencies for escape, relying on a buddy to drive a getaway car. But the car was nowhere to be seen when they exited the bank; a delivery truck had blocked the street, causing a traffic snarl. The men split up. One of the robbers was caught a block from the bank, trying to hail a cab, a bag of money in his hand. The other two were caught within the hour.

He was sitting in a bus, facing sideways, east toward the river. The city and the river confused him. He thought he understood the streets, but the river ballooned out away from the highway, and suddenly brand new streets with unfamiliar names came at him. According to the SEPTA map he had picked up in the hotel lobby, this bus made a loop, from the center of town toward the northeast part of the city and then back again. It would take him to within a block of the transfer station. He checked his watch. It was actually on time, according to the schedule. If it continued to be on time, the schedule would tell him when to expect a return bus.

It was a spectacular day. The sun was so bright that it even penetrated the filth on the bus's windows. Evans appreciated good weather, although he wouldn't choose to spend it in a city unless he was working.

He checked his watch. Since the bus was on time, he would be very early if he exited the bus and walked to the transfer station. If he rode the bus back into town, he might be late. He looked carefully through the dirty windows. There was a decent-looking restaurant sitting incongruously among the warehouses, advertising local beers on tap and crabs. He rang the bell on the bus, and left at the next stop. He walked back to the restaurant. He wasn't hungry, but he could make a beer last an hour, and then he could walk over for his meeting with Old Rick. The old bastard would undoubtedly regale him with tales of the perfidy of his family. Larry Evans could be a good listener.

He almost hesitated at the restaurant door; two police cruisers were idling in the parking lot. But he was in control of himself, and he continued into the restaurant without a pause. He waved at the hostess and headed for the bar. The place smelled of spilled beer and crab seasoning, a not unpleasant smell. He sat on a backless stool and ordered a Yards ale.

As the bartender was drawing his beer, Evans thought about what it might mean to have the cops so close to the area he needed for his work. He hadn't considered that the police could be a presence in the neighborhood, which was industrial and mostly rundown. It was one thing for the cops to make random sweeps around the streets; it was another for two carsful of cops to linger a block from what would soon be a murder scene.

Larry Evans decided he needed to have alternative methods at hand. He checked his watch, drank his beer, paid and left. He started walking toward the river.

He was relieved to discover that the bus and the restaurant, as well as the cops cooping in the parking lot, were much farther from the transfer station than it looked on the map. One block on the map was actually more like a half mile, with cul-de-sac alleys sitting where streets would have been if the area had been residential. He turned around and walked backwards for a few steps, then resumed his forward march. He had no doubt that the cops were close enough to hear a gunshot if the wind was blowing in off the river, and if they were paying attention, and if no traffic noises interfered. He wouldn't take the chance. A gun was out.

He felt very pleased with himself. He had turned some potentially bad news into some good intel. He could accomplish his mission successfully. He walked on toward the river, and toward his date with the abusive old man.

Chapter 24

We are all the heroes of our own story, the protagonist in a cosmic television show. When I was a kid I used to think my life was being filmed from above. So we look at the world through the lens of "me, me, me."

Which is why the situation with the Barnards ticked me off—they were bugging me. I didn't really care that they were also bugging each other. I didn't really care that they wanted to expand their business, except to the extent it would mean more work for me and my firm. Of course, I care about Monica, and her happiness, but perhaps that is because she is a product of me, me, me.

And then when Two-face came to my office, I was ready to explode, since he wanted to talk about the Barnards.

As I've probably made clear, he isn't one of my favorite people, and his need to discuss two more of my not-favorite people seemed to be adding insult to injury.

"Jack, how are you," he said, looking at me and over my shoulder at the same time. He sat in one of my guest chairs.

"Great, Ron," I said. "And you?"

"Great, great," he said.

He looked at me with his right eye, then his left.

"I've been asked by the FUC to talk to you about your clients, the Barnards."

"Go ahead," I said.

"Well, it's come to our attention that you've turned away some business from Mrs. Barnard."

I waited for him to go on. As a lawyer, I know the value of not rushing into speech.

"Are you denying that?" he said.

"No," I said.

Again, I waited for him to speak.

"Well, Jack, your partners deserve an explanation," he said.

"My explanation is that we were conflicted out of the representation," I said.

I hoped that my use of fancy lawyer language, which boiled down to "we can't represent both sides in a dispute," would impress him. But it didn't.

"There is almost always a way to finesse a conflict situation," Ron said. "You should have come to me to talk it through."

"My own personal sense of honor required me to back off, Ron, and coming to you to "finesse" the situation wouldn't have withstood my own sense of how to handle it."

Ron's face began to redden. He continued to stare at my face and my left shoulder.

"Are you accusing me of something?" he said.

"I'm just explaining myself," I said.

"Let me be frank with you," said Ron.

"Please Ron," I said, "be frank."

He narrowed his eyes.

"I don't think your attempt to be funny is successful," he said.

"I was amusing myself, Ron, and I enjoyed it," I said.

He stood up suddenly.

"You will talk to the Barnards about using us for the litigation and the transactions they're looking to pursue, and you will appear before the FUC at next week's meeting to tell us you've done it."

I looked at Ron's nose, which was the easiest thing for me to focus on, and thought about the fact that I was twenty years his senior and could most probably sway the Barnards away from the firm entirely, if I was so inclined.

"Why should I?" I said. "What's in it for me?"

His eyes popped out of his head, both at slightly different angles, and he gritted his teeth.

"Just do it," he said. "Or there will be consequences."

He strode out of my office before I could respond. Which was probably just as well, since my retort was something juvenile, along the lines of "ooooh, I'm so scared!"

Because, really, what's the worst that could happen?

Chapter 25

Old Rick let Larry Evans into the office, which was empty of people.

"Upstairs," he said. "Drinks in the upstairs conference room."

Old Rick had obviously gotten a head start. The smell of metabolized alcohol was seeping from his pores, and his tread was unsteady. Evans checked his watch. It was barely five p.m.

"Office closes at 5?" said Larry Evans.

Old Rick glanced over his shoulder.

"Four thirty," he said. "After the second shift drivers come in."

Larry Evans nodded as if he knew what the old man was saying. His nod went unnoticed, however. The old man was plodding to the back of the building, toward a set of steep stairs.

Larry was glad he was fit. The stairs wound around twice. Old Rick, surprisingly, had no trouble with the stairs.

"Here," he said. He pointed to a big open space with a makeshift bar, and bottles of every imaginable kind of liquor cramming bookshelves. It was just the two of them.

Larry wondered if the old man had a premonition of some kind. This would be a perfect opportunity to fulfill his job orders, except for the fact that he hadn't yet been given the final go-ahead.

Old Rick reinforced Evans' thoughts when he produced, in his left hand, an empty martini glass, and in his right, a revolver. He held them evenly balanced, as if weighing whether to have a drink or fire the gun.

Larry Evans let consternation show on his face.

He put both his hands up toward his shoulders, palm up. See, I'm no threat.

"Want a martoonie?" Old Rick said. He still held the glass and the pistol.

"Sure, especially after having you wave that around," Larry Evans said.

"Well, you're a cowboy, aren't you? Thought you'd like to see this old six shooter."

Old Rick handed the pistol to Larry Evans, butt end first, chuckled, and then headed to the bar, which was a plank across the top of a low bookcase.

Larry Evans examined the handgun. It was a Colt Revolver, and it looked as though it was in pristine condition despite a serial number that seemed to put it as a 19th century piece. He noted that the chambers were all full.

He put the gun on the bar.

"Use it much?" he said.

"Nope. It was my grandfather's. Sometimes I shoot cans out in the back of the place."

"I guess you keep it loaded in case you need to shoot a can," said Larry Evans.

The old man laughed.

"Gin or vodka?" he said.

"Only one way to have a real martini," said Evans. "Gin. Cold. No vermouth."

"Hey, I like that," said Old Rick. He poured half a bottle of Beefeater's into a cocktail shaker, threw in some ice sitting in a bucket, and shook the shaker.

Then he poured a huge drink for Evans, and an equally large one for himself.

"Take a drink of that," he said, "and then you and I have some talking to do."

Evans sipped his drink. It was excellent.

"Nice," he said. "Icy."

"You got it," said Old Rick. "Okay, here's the deal. My good-for-nothing family wants me to sell my business. I don't want to. I know you represent the potential buyer. So, here's the scoop: no deal. I have nothing against you. I'm just not selling. End of story."

He took a large swallow of his martini.

"Is it my turn now?" said Larry Evans. He smiled to take the edge off the comment. "Because you did say WE had some talking to do, and you just made me a speech."

Old Rick gestured with his martini hand.

"Go ahead," he said. "Say your piece."

"I've heard you're a good businessman, and my guess is that your speech is just the opening position in your game."

Old Rick laughed. "You heard that, did you?" he said.

"Yup, I did."

"Well, I am a good businessman, a really good negotiator," he said. "But this isn't a negotiation. I'm telling you and whoever you represent to drop dead. I'm not interested."

Larry Evans stared at Old Rick. He had to be sure this was for real.

"You haven't even heard our final offer," he said.

"Doesn't matter," said Old Rick. "I'm not selling out. I'm not selling for love or money. Forget it. And if I didn't like you, I'd tell you to go to hell. I might still tell you that if you don't leave me alone."

"Are you really telling me that you won't sell?"

"I won't sell," said Old Rick. "And I've been telling my good-for-nothing relatives the same thing. Over my dead body."

Larry Evans nodded. He could make sure that Old Rick would get what he wanted.

Larry Evans raised his martini glass. "Here's to you, old man," he said.

Chapter 26

I thought that Two-Face was simply blowing smoke. Since his implied threat was so unspecific, and since I was a full senior partner in the firm—an owner—I couldn't imagine what the Firm Underwriting Committee could possibly do to me. I discovered, as events unfolded, that my imagination isn't as robust as it should be.

I am reminded of the long ago U.S. Senate hearings on Clarence Thomas's nomination to the Supreme Court. Whether or not you believed his accuser, who said he behaved inappropriately and sexually harassed her, is irrelevant. He was confirmed, and added his own brand of conservatism to the Court.

No, what's relevant to my thinking is Justice Thomas's complaint that he was the victim of a "high-tech lynching," meaning he believed that his accusers were motivated by racial hatred, but that they would stop short of physically lynching him. Although I'm not a member of a racial minority, the use of technology to undo a man is not limited to Supreme Court justices.

So when I started reading my emails the next morning, I was startled to see my name in the "subject" section of approximately twenty messages.

The Firm Underwriting Committee had started the ball rolling by sending all partners a notice that a special meeting was being called to oust me from the firm. The Board claimed the ouster was required because of my undermining of the firm's financial success.

The emails responding to the FUC's notice were, as one would expect from lawyers, not so much supportive as hyper-technical. A number of my partners demanded to know what part of the partnership agreement would permit such an unusual step. Eldon, ever the wit, asked if the firm should remove my photo from the firm website before the universe crashed around us. In law firms, this is what passes for support.

I have to admit I had a bad feeling in the pit of my gut. No one likes to be hated, and the fact that our FUC had made a personal attack on me hurt my feelings. It also made me incredibly angry.

If this had happened when I was young and energetic, I would have fought my partners. The thought, though, of marshaling support, talking to my partners about "keeping" me, filled me with deep weariness. I realized with something of a shock that I really didn't care enough to do anything about what appeared to be an ignominious end to my legal career.

My train of thought led me to call Catherine King, not to hurry along toward getting me an appointment to talk to this dream law firm, but rather to cancel whatever she had set up. I was too old for this.

"Hey, Jack," she said. "I was going to call you. I have a few dates for you to meet with these new folks."

"Actually, Catherine, I've decided that I've had it with law firms."

"Now what?" she said.

I gave her a brief synopsis.

"Those jerks," she said. "But it's just business as usual. Why take it personally now?"

"Life is too short," I said. "And thanks for thinking of me."

She tried to convince me to meet with "the new folks," but I was adamant. We hung up on good terms. I promised to call her if I changed my mind.

I felt curiously relieved after my call with Catherine. I had said it aloud: I've had it with law firms. I had made a decision, it seemed, and the idea that I could stop fighting the inevitable drained away my exhaustion and my anger. I was free.

Eldon chose that moment to knock on my door. I waved him into my office, and he sat on a guest chair.

"So," he said, "the shit has hit the fan. And I guess you're the fan."

"It's fair to say that I'm certainly not the shit— that honor goes to Two-face. And I'm no longer a fan."

"He's out of control," Eldon said.

"Of course, I agree with you," I said. "But he's brought the entire FUC down the same road with him."

"Like Hitler rallying the troops," he said.

"If I repeat the Hitler remark," I said, "you'll wind up on the street as well."

"I know you won't repeat it," he said. "That's why I knew I could say it."

He looked searchingly at me.

"You won't repeat it, right?"

I looked at his stricken face, which had turned a pale grey, and laughed.

"No, you have nothing to worry about," I said.

"I think I'll have to keep looking over my shoulder now that Two-face has decided to p-p-play rough," he said.

Ron walked by my office, stopped to glare at me and at Eldon, one with each eye, and continued to move away. Although Eldon hadn't turned around, he seemed to sense that Ron had been there.

"I hope he d-d-didn't hear me," Eldon said.

"I don't think he did," I said. "Try not to worry."

"I better get out of here," he said. "Guilt by association."

He stood up and scuttled out of my office, after looking both ways to see who could see him emerging.

I decided to take a walk, to see how many of my partners would talk to me. Not to politic, mind you, just to talk. It was stupid. I shouldn't have. It just made me feel bad. Every senior lawyer in the firm avoided my gaze, each suddenly very absorbed in some other task—getting a soda from the fridge, pouring coffee, talking on the phone, talking to each other.

The craziest part of all of this was that just weeks ago, I had been lauded for bringing in the Barnards as clients in the first place, years ago. I was set up on a pedestal as an example of how to bring in business to some of the younger lawyers. Now I was just getting set up.

I saw Donald, the former chair of the litigation department, out of the corner of my eye. He gestured to me to follow him, and he pointed to the file room. At least he hadn't motioned me into a broom closet.

"What the hell is going on?" he said. He spoke in a husky whisper.

"What do you mean?" I said.

He shushed me, and flapped his hand, to encourage me to whisper, too.

"What is it with the FUC?" he said. "They've been taken over by aliens. You're one of the biggest business producers in the firm. Why piss you off?"

"Well, Donald," I said, "why piss you off? You're well known in the legal community as a great educator and lawyer. That makes no sense, either."

I was speaking softly, but apparently not softly enough for Donald. He moved closer to me, and started to whisper into my face. His breath was awful. This was truly going to be torture.

"Jack, if you leave with all your clients, the firm is going to lose a lot of business."

He was whispering into my nose, and I turned my head as if to hear him better. My ear has no receptors for smell.

"What's going on?" he said.

I shrugged my shoulders.

"Power grab, I guess," I said, into his ear. "They can whack up the pie into fewer pieces."

A secretary entered the file room, to find us intimately entwined as I tried to keep Donald's breath out of my face. Her eyes widened, and she turned around and left.

"Let's get out of here," I said.

Donald threw up his hands and left. I followed. The scared secretary was busily whispering to her new best friends, all the secretaries sitting near the file room. They all looked at me as I walked down the hall.

When I reached my office, I closed the door behind me, and started to giggle. Yes, this was serious, but it was so stupid! I tried to keep my giggles quiet, so as not to alarm anyone, and I wound up crying.

The truth was, I didn't want to leave the firm with my clients. I had been intending to transition the clients to various firm lawyers, as I retired into a life of golf and writing. Leaving the firm with my clients and establishing myself and them in a new home took work, and I was trying to exit the working life. What a mess.

I hadn't signed up for this. And I wanted to sign out.

Chapter 27

There was a message waiting for Larry Evans when he returned to his hotel. The message light was blinking on his phone. He headed for the minibar before he retrieved it, topping off his martini buzz with a Coke. He rubbed his eyes, shook his head, and then picked up the receiver.

"Hey," said the familiar voice. "Call me. I think I have the instruction you've been waiting for. And possibly some new business."

Larry Evans hung up the phone, put down his Coke, and decided to take a cold shower. He wasn't drunk, but he wasn't completely clear-headed, either. He wanted to have all synapses firing when he talked to his handler.

The water was cold enough to elicit a strangled grunt from him. The first moment made him want to leave the bathroom and take a nap. He forced himself to stay under the spray. As his skin began to cool, his brain began to wake up. After ten minutes of this self-torture, he turned off the shower, toweled off, and put his clothes back on.

Perhaps the passing years had lowered his tolerance for alcohol. He was still angry with himself for killing the hooker. What was the point? The risk was unnecessary, and he had allowed himself to lose control. Neither was good for his chosen profession. If he decided to give up alcohol, could he do it on his own, or would he be forced to join AA? Would he meet other professional killers? Perhaps there exists an AA specifically for killers. That would be helpful.

He stopped himself from coming up with ridiculous scenarios involving a room full of alcoholic killers, regaling each other with how the demon drink had interfered with their professional lives. He needed to get on with his work.

He returned the phone call.

"Ah, there you are," said his contact. "Where have you been?"

"Drinking with the target," said Evans.

"Well, you'll be happy to hear that you've been given the go-ahead."

Evans waited.

"Eliminate the target."

"OK," Evans said.

"You don't seem to be able to operate on subtleties," his contact said.

"I only operate on clear orders," Evans said. "You know that."

He heard a sigh on the other end.

"Yes," said his contact.

"And you said there was more work?"

"Yes, but let's complete this project first."

"Whatever you say," said Evans. "Am I leaving town after completion?"

"No, call me for further instructions. You're to stay in place."

"OK," said Evans. He hung up the phone.

Time to get some food into his system.

Chapter 28

It occurred to me that there was only one way the Firm Underwriting Committee could have heard about my refusal to take on Mrs. Barnard's business. She, the old bat, must have called one of my partners to complain. That, however, didn't explain the newly-devised vendetta against me. Perhaps the FUC members were bored and had decided to FUC with me.

I did have a suspicion, however, that the entire brouhaha was manufactured as a way of keeping all the troops in line. If enough people feared reprisals, no one would vote against the FUC's proposals. The FUC could even propose that certain partners receive less money, and if the fear was strong enough, everyone would acquiesce. I had certainly read about big law firms like ours turning on their partners in order to share the pie among fewer mouths.

What I couldn't figure out was why they didn't just let me be. I was slated for retirement. They would have been through with me soon enough.

I looked up to see Two-face at my door. His eyes, despite pointing in opposite directions, glowed with hatred. Then he turned and walked away. I realized that he was fucking with me because he could. That explained a lot. I was determined not to rise to any of his bait.

I had the phone handset in my hand to thank my daughter for dinner when Two-face reappeared. I replaced the receiver in the cradle.

"We're moving your office," he said to me.

"What do you mean?"

Despite my new self-imposed resolution not to let him get to me, I was instantly angry.

"We're moving you to the fourth floor," he said. "Next to Hazan Ahkbar."

I felt as though I was frothing at the mouth. Hazan was the head of the firm's technology department. No lawyers had offices on that floor.

I drew a deep breath.

"No, you're not," I said.

And I picked up the phone. I shooed him out of my office with a wave of the hand, and pointedly ignored his efforts to speak to me. I pretended to dial a client, although I was actually dialing my own home number, so that I could stop trying to figure out which eye was looking my way. And I was too upset to call my daughter. Two-face finally departed.

I put down the phone. All this nonsense was leading me to the inevitable conclusion: it was time to leave the firm. I hated the idea of leaving on someone else's schedule, but such is life.

A new face appeared at my door. It was David Smith, head of operations.

"Ron tells me you're moving your office," he said.

"I'm not," I said.

"Oh," he said. He continued standing at my door.

I said no more, and he shrugged his shoulders and left.

What a rotten day this was becoming.

Chapter 29

Larry Evans sat on his bed and mentally reviewed his inventory. This job would go better up close and personal. He was always concerned about how far sound travels, and a gunshot was asking for trouble. It meant he might have to sacrifice a tool to do it, but it would be altogether cleaner.

He stood up to open his suitcase, and opened the door to the closet. He froze. It wasn't there. He felt his heart begin to pound. He whirled around to scan the room. He didn't see his suitcase. Instead, he saw, on the floor, just inside the door to the room, the "Do Not Disturb" sign he had put on the outside door handle. It had fallen off, and his room had been cleaned. In fact, clearly, his room had been disturbed.

He forced himself to breathe deeply and to slow his heart rate. He scanned the room again. No suitcase. He turned on all the lights, and entered the closet. His clothes were there, but there was no suitcase. He dropped to one knee and looked under the bed. This was one of the few hotels that actually vacuumed under the bed. No dust bunnies, and no suitcase.

He stood up and strode to the bathroom. He didn't expect to find his case there, but he was mistaken. It sat just beside the door to the bathroom, on a folding luggage rack, in a small niche whose purpose had eluded him. He tried the locks, and was relieved to see it was still locked. He cursed the room cleaner for being too much of an activist. As his heart rate returned to normal, he began to laugh at himself. He rubbed his eyes, and opened the case.

He found the pieces to the garrote, and rolled them carefully so they would fit into an inside pocket of his jacket. He checked himself in the mirror, and was satisfied that the bulge wasn't too conspicuous. He thought it was time to call his good buddy Old Rick for another round of drinks. And he would insist that they meet tonight.

Chapter 30

One of our senior associates, who looked to be about twelve, walked by my office, towing behind him an even younger-looking man. Our internecine warfare obviously had not trickled down to the staff, because the twelve-year old entered my office and introduced me to his young charge.

"Jack is one of the many good guys around here," the senior associate said.

Unbeknownst to him, he was currying favor with the wrong partner.

"Our firm has a 'no jerks' rule," the associate said. "So this is a great place to work."

"Oh," said the two-year old job seeker.

He was not a master of small talk. Then he remembered his manners.

"Nice meeting you," he said.

As they left, I laughed. I admit I laughed bitterly, but that's better than not laughing at all. Our firm has a "no jerks" rule, my ass.

My phone rang. In a Pavlovian response, I immediately picked up the handset. Before I had a chance to regret it, I said hello. Much to my delight, it was Monica.

"Hi, Dad," she said. "Did I catch you at a bad time?"

I toyed with telling her the truth, and rejected that option.

"Not at all," I said. "I'm always available to talk to you."

"You are such a gooshball," she said.

"I know," I said. "What's up?"

"Just a coincidence I wanted to share," she said. "You know that property I was telling you about, near the river?"

"I remember," I said.

"I just realized that Barnard Hardware is your client. They're across from the transfer station."

"I know," I said.

"Small world, huh?"

Something was off here. I could not believe Monica was just calling for a "small world" discussion.

"Monica," I said.

I heard her sigh.

"My boss wanted me to talk to you about the Barnard Hardware site."

Good to know that conflicts of interest arise even on the side of the "good guys."

"What did he want you to say?"

"His political contacts told him that Barnard Hardware might be considering a purchase of the transfer station property."

"I guess your boss hangs out at the Famous," I said.

The Famous was a deli in what used to be the garment district of Philadelphia. It sat in the midst of a gentrified neighborhood now known as Queen Village. And all the city's movers and shakers met for breakfast there every morning, unless they had a conflict. A concerned citizen could learn a lot about what was going on in Philadelphia by sitting near their long table.

"Yes," she said. She sighed again.

"What can I help you with?" I said.

"He would like a confirmation of this rumor," she said.

"Well, since he's the government, can't he just call and ask the Barnards, or the folks who own the transfer station?"

"He tried that. Both property owners refused to talk to him."

I laughed. I could imagine old Mrs. Barnard slamming the phone down in response to a question she didn't want to answer.

"Well, sweetie, you know I can't reveal a client confidence," I said.

"I know, but I promised I'd ask," she said.

"Okay," I said. "You asked."

There was an awkward silence, and then we both said some nonsense about getting back to work, and got off the phone. Those damn Barnards. Their existence supports my mantra: clients, can't live without 'em, can't live with 'em.

I looked up as a shadow loomed. It was David Smith again.

"I'm here to pack up your office," he said. "Ron's orders."

"David, go to hell," I said.

David turned beet red.

"How dare you talk to me like that?" he said. "Apologize."

"Are you nuts?" I said.

I stood up.

"I'm one of your bosses. Get out of my office."

I started toward him. His eyes bugged out of his head.

"You'll regret this," he said.

He stood his ground. And I walked right past him, out the door of my office.

He turned toward me.

"Get back here," he said. "Don't you dare turn your back on me."

I kept walking. It seemed to me that the inmates had finally taken over the asylum.

Chapter 31

Old Rick was tickled pink that Larry wanted to hoist a few with him. When Larry walked in the door, Old Rick greeted him like a long-lost friend, pounding him on the back.

"No hard feelings, right?" said Old Rick.

"None," said Larry Evans.

"Come on back to the bar," Old Rick said.

He motioned to the hallway, and waved Larry on.

They started to walk down the hall.

"Where is everyone?" Larry said.

"All gone home."

"Really? Not even a janitor?"

"All gone," Old Rick said.

"No one wanted to join us for a drink?"

"I didn't tell anyone you were coming in," Old Rick said.

Larry stopped.

"You know," Larry said, "before we have a drink, would you do me a favor?"

Old Rick looked suspicious.

"What?" he said.

"I'd like to see the transfer station. Up close and personal. Even though I know you're not selling."

"Is this a trick?"

"No trick," said Larry. "Just curiosity."

Old Rick reversed direction, and squeezed past Larry, moving toward the office door.

"Come on," he said.

"Will I get to see some trash being dumped?"

"Nope. We close the station after 6. Our people are long gone."

"Too bad," said Larry. "I was hoping to see how everything works."

"I'll show you," said Old Rick. "I know every inch of this place, and every gear and screw."

They walked toward the huge shed. There were trash trucks around it, neatly parked in parallel lines. Larry patted the pocket that held the garrote. He had polished the bracelets so that no DNA or fingerprints remained. He had wrapped two gloves around the garrote.

Old Rick waved toward the shed.

"We lower the door when we're done for the night," he said. "Keeps birds away. Also keeps the environmentalists away."

He laughed.

"Condition of our permit," he said.

He walked to a panel on the wall of the shed, and punched in a code. Larry saw it, and inwardly grinned. 1-2-3-4 was pretty easy to remember.

The huge door began to roll upward. Larry thought it wasn't possible for the stench to be worse than it was outside the shed, but he was wrong. A wall of smell assailed them.

Old Rick smiled. "Great smell, huh?" he said. He went to a panel of switches on the wall, and turned on overhead lights that made it seem like high noon.

Larry began to rethink his strategy. Even a motorist passing blocks away would be able to see into the shed now.

But Old Rick surprised him. He tapped 1-2-3-4 into a wall panel, and the huge door began to roll down.

"Don't want the neighbors complaining," he said. "Especially that bitch Barnard across the road."

Larry smiled. He stepped closer to Rick, and watched carefully as Rick turned toward the deep concrete pit half filled with garbage.

"The trucks bring the garbage in here," Old Rick said. He gestured to the pit.

"Then when it's full, we compact it. Takes up less landfill space." He pointed to a long lever on the wall. "That arm operates the rams," he said.

Larry nodded.

"Can you show me?" he said.

"Sure," Old Rick said. He marched over to the lever. He pulled it down, and the walls of the pit began to move inward, compressing the trash sitting there.

Larry started to modify his plan. Couldn't the old man just fall into the pit? And if the compacter was working, wouldn't he be squashed like a bug? The simplicity of the thing appealed to him.

Rick reversed the direction of the rams. "No point in compacting what's there," he said. "Not enough to make a difference. We'll wait until the morning deliveries to do it."

Larry nodded. "Fascinating," he said.

Rick came back over to the edge of the pit.

"Simple as can be," Rick said. "Gather up everyone's garbage, smash it into a smaller space, take it to a landfill, and make a lot of money." He laughed.

Larry knocked into the old man, elbowing him in the ribs but otherwise not touching him.

"Hey!" Old Rick said.

Larry stuck out his cowboy boot and swept Old Rick's feet out from under him, hitting him again in the ribs with an elbow.

"What the fuck," Old Rick said. He slowly toppled over into the pit, unable to keep his footing.

"Sorry, old man," said Larry. He walked over to the lever, and pushed it downward. He heard the rams begin to engage. He walked over to the pit. Old Rick was lying on the pile of garbage, trying to get his footing, breathing hard, and screaming. The rams moved relentlessly toward him. He faced up toward Larry, on his hands and knees. He didn't scream any more. He looked resigned.

Larry watched with interest as the rams approached the old man. He saw Old Rick close his eyes. There was little resistance to hold the rams back, as there wasn't much in the way of garbage to protect Old Rick. The old man took one big breath, and screamed as the rams crushed his ribs. He couldn't scream any more, then. Larry saw blood seep from Old Rick's nose and mouth. His mouth was forming a noiseless "O."

Larry waited until the old man wasn't breathing. Then he waited another 20 minutes. Then he reversed the rams, and watched as Old Rick's body took an unnatural position on the top of the garbage pile. For good measure, he waited another 20 minutes. He liked to be thorough. He put his surgical gloves on and then he turned out the overhead lights, and punched the code into the panel on the wall.

The air outside the shed was better than inside, but not by much. Before the giant door had finished its upward travels, he hit the outside panel with the code, and the door started to travel down. When it was shut, Larry looked around to see if the noise had awakened a neighbor or alerted the cops. As his eyes adjusted to the dark, he felt himself completely alone. He saw no one.

Larry Evans smiled. Another job well done. And he hadn't even had to use any of his bag of tricks.

The driver of the white Cadillac waited until Evans was out of sight, then rolled quietly out of the parking area and onto the street.

Chapter 32

The fact that one of my employees had decided I was no longer entitled to the respect due a partner in the firm told me volumes. At the least, word was out that the FUC wanted me out of the firm. At the worst, the FUC had spread lies and rumors that caused the staff to believe I was a monster.

I have noticed that when people behave badly, they must manufacture a reason for doing it. Even sociopaths seem to need to create a rationale for their actions. No one in my experience has simply said "I don't want to share my money with you anymore." Instead, they say "Your attitude is hurting the firm's integrity." This of course is true everywhere in the working world, not just among lawyers. I believe it is one of the least attractive traits of our species.

After I walked out of my office and into the world, I went directly home and made myself a gigantic gin martini, icy cold with no vermouth. After half of it, I was able to think about dinner, and after I had consumed the entire drink, I was no longer conscious, so eating wasn't an option. I woke up the next morning stiff from sleeping on the sofa in an upright position, starved and thirsty.

During my self-induced coma, I had apparently come to a conclusion: I'd absolutely had it with the firm and I didn't want to be there anymore. Even if it meant I had to leave behind all of my belongings and even if I didn't get another cent from those bastards, I wasn't going back.

As I ate a hearty breakfast of eggs and sausage and toast, and drank a quart of orange juice and a gallon of coffee, I began to plan the reality of my life going forward. Transforming myself into something other than a lawyer seemed impossible. And yet the idea that my firm, where I had practiced for most of my adult life, was most likely no different from any other firm, put a damper on any thoughts about simply moving my practice.

It suddenly occurred to me to call Monica. She is a beacon of sanity. She might have some advice for her old man.

Monica was surprised to hear from me so early in the day.

"Hi, Dad, what's going on?"

I explained to her as succinctly as I could about my life, my career, my disaffection for the firm, and my decision to leave. Succinct, in this case, took about an hour. To Monica's credit, she didn't interrupt me, didn't sigh, didn't say she had to go.

"Maybe I should become a government lawyer," I said. "You seem very happy where you are."

"Dad," said Monica, "sometimes you are such a girl."

I laughed in spite of myself.

"What do you mean?"

"The world of work is nasty and brutish," she said. "It doesn't matter where you are. There are always psychopaths and back-stabbers in every organization."

"Who taught you that?" I said.

"No one. I learned it over time. And it helps to have a group of other women lawyers to talk to, like my lunch group."

I remembered her lunch group. She had told me about finding six other like-minded women who met for lunch every week. A modern support group.

"Monica, I cannot believe that other organizations put up with lying, cheating, gossiping, and undercutting in the ways I've just told you about."

"That's why I say you're such a girl sometimes. Women always believe that merit will be rewarded. It isn't always."

I felt the irony of having my sweet daughter explain the miseries of the world to me.

"You've given me a lot to think about," I said. "Thank you, I guess."

Monica laughed. "You're welcome, Daddy," she said.

My head was reeling. Of course, I knew she was right. I had lulled myself into a false sense of security because for so many years everything at the firm had been great for me. I had been an ostrich, failing to lift my head out of the sand long enough to notice which lawyers had been dissed or had their draws reduced. And how could I forget the examples of my clients, the Barnards? In-fighting and meanness brought to a full boil. Monica was right. Not only was I a girl, I was a Pollyanna.

Which really made my decision about what to do next both easy and hard. Easy, because I realized I would have to work for myself to avoid the madness of the workplace. Hard, because I had no idea what that work would be. What was I going to do with the rest of my life?

Chapter 33

Larry Evans walked the mile from the transfer station to the bus terminal. Halogen lights lit up the terminal, showing an assortment of working folks, bus drivers, police officers and street people. Apart from his cowboy boots, he fit right into the hodge-podge. He sat on a bench, waiting for the bus that he knew would take him back into center city, near his hotel. A young kid toting a guitar and wearing cowboy boots passed in front of him. He silently thanked the gods of footwear. Now there was even less to make him stand out in the crowd.

His plan to handle Old Rick had been simple. Either he'd dispose of him at the transfer station, or he'd throw his body in the river. He expected that Rick's body would be found either way. There was nothing to tie him to the killing, although it nagged at him that he'd been forced to play a role, forced to meet old Rick's family, and forced to stick around for another job. These things made him vulnerable to suspicion, if not to proof.

Of course, he really wasn't being "forced" to do anything. He could decline the job that was holding him here. In fact, the more he thought about it, the more it made sense. He should get out while he could. He decided to deliver the message to his contact tonight. Then he would get out of Dodge.

As the bus for Center City pulled into the terminal, he stood to get in line. Jesus, he was getting old, he thought. For some reason, every bone in his body hurt. He found himself limping along the line, and taking the steps into the bus was agony. Another good reason to get back to his ranch. The northeastern air was killing him.

By the time he got off at his stop, he was feeling ill enough to consider going to a hospital. This was not good. He wanted to leave as few tell-tales as possible, and checking into an emergency room was asking for trouble. Was he Larry Evans, with no insurance? If he checked in as himself, he was screwed.

He limped off toward the hotel. Maybe a good night's sleep would repair what ailed him. By the time he got to his room, he was sweating profusely, and he wondered if he'd make it to his room. But he did. And he had the presence of mind to put a "don't bother me" sign on the door handle. His phone was ringing, but he ignored it.

He fell on the bed, fully clothed, face down, and passed out. Just before sinking into a coma-like darkness, he wondered if the old man had poisoned him.

He awoke an hour later, drenched in sweat, his clothes sodden. He managed to turn over on his back, bent his knees, and tugged off one boot at a time. The effort exhausted him, and despite the phone ringing again, he plunged back into his dreamless coma.

Another hour passed, and another emerging into the light, long enough to realize the phone had been ringing on and off the entire time, and with enough energy to pull off his water-logged clothes, pull back the bed covers, and collapse onto the sheets. The next time he awoke, it was the next morning. And he was ravenous.

He laughed at himself. Rarely a drama queen, he had imagined old Rick poisoning him, when all he had was a common twenty-four hour virus. The aging process was getting to his brain. He got up to shower, and his phone rang. His handler could wait another hour before talking to him. Larry was going to get clean, have a big breakfast, and then talk to the man. It was the least he could do for himself.

Chapter 34

I spent a leisurely morning at home, drinking pots of coffee and reading the paper. I definitely could see myself not hustling into an office anymore. What would I miss about the practice of law?

I made a mental list, too lazy to get up to get a pencil and paper.

I would miss my good clients, as people.

I would miss the challenge of advising my clients on ways to accomplish their goals.

I would miss having a secretary.

That was it. A pretty short list.

I needed to come up with an activity that would put me in touch with people, and allow me to continue to use my brain to help people navigate whatever needed navigating. I could live without a secretary.

The caffeine was definitely helping me to think coherently. Cogently. Unfortunately, none of that helped me figure out exactly what new role in life would suit me.

I thought about my very enjoyable dinner with Monica, where she picked my brain. If I could make money sitting with someone I like, solving problems, I would do it in a heartbeat.

Then I mentally slapped myself in the head. I had enough money saved to never have to work again in my life. I could give away my expertise.

But then would anyone value my advice? Free advice can also be worthless advice.

My phone rang. I looked at the readout. It was Mrs. Barnard. I briefly considered not picking it up, but I realized that since she had my home phone number, she could bug me nonstop for many days.

"Mrs. Barnard, hello," I said.

"How did you know it was me?"

I explained the workings of the modern phone to her.

"How can I help you?" I said.

"My nemesis is dead," she said.

That brought me up short. First, that she made the reference to nemesis. She was perhaps more well read than I thought. Then, because I didn't know if she meant her son.

"Who?" I said. "What?"

"Old Rick Kozak," she said. "Found dead. At his transfer station across the street."

She sounded very cheerful about it.

"He was the SOB who wouldn't sell. With him gone, my chance to expand here is a reality."

It was probably time to call the "uh oh" squad. She certainly did seem to be still running her company. And Stanley?

"How is Stanley with all this?" I said.

"Stanley is a jerk," she said. "He doesn't want to take on the environmental liability. He has no foresight."

"Why are you calling me, Mrs. Barnard?"

"Because I've instructed my lawyer to call you as a witness in my lawsuit with Stanley."

"What? Why?"

"You can explain that I was the one who came to you with the idea of buying out the transfer station. That Stanley was against it."

My head began to hurt.

"This is such a bad idea," I said. "I can't testify to anything that will help you."

"You'll be hearing from my lawyer," she said.

"Mrs. Barnard, I know you had an interest in the property, but I know nothing about Stanley's position on it."

"Now you know. I just told you so."

"I can't do it," I said. "I won't lie."

"I have no such hesitation," she said. "I'll report you to the Ethics Board."

"For what, refusing to lie?"

"No, I'll tell them you offered to support Stanley unless I paid you a bribe."

I was so glad I had decided to stop representing the Barnards.

"Mrs. Barnard," I said, "do what you have to do."

And I hung up.

Chapter 35

Larry Evans felt much better after a big breakfast and a shower. Almost as though he'd never gotten sick. It must have been a short-lived virus.

He called his handler.

"What the fuck!" his handler said. "Where the fuck have you been?"

"Worried about me?" Evans said.

"Let's say angry," his handler said.

"It's nice of you to worry. I was actually on death's door, but I'm okay. Now what?"

"Mission accomplished?"

"Yeah, for real."

"This next one is related to last night's."

"I'm not so sure that's a good idea," said Evans. "If family members start dropping like flies, the cops might figure it out."

"Not related, like family. Related like, same business deal."

"Then I have the same problem."

His handler was silent.

"I heard last night's was clean," he said. "It was written up in the paper as an accident—drunk firm founder falls into his own trash compactor."

"It was clean," Evans said. "But if another person suddenly drops dead who's part of the deal, someone's bound to get suspicious."

"Here's the good news—Larry Evans can disappear. You don't need to play a role. Just get near the target and get rid of him."

"What if someone recognizes me?"

"Most likely won't happen."

"That doesn't make me feel warm and fuzzy."

"Listen, you're a pro. You know how to be invisible. Just do it. There's a bonus because of the risk."

"Call me tomorrow at this time," Evans said. "Use my cell. I have to ditch Larry Evans and this nice hotel."

"Deal," said his contact.

Larry Evans sat on his hotel bed to consider his options. His Larry Evans persona had outlasted its purpose. What were the pros and cons of keeping himself as Larry Evans? The biggest negative was that if Larry Evans was still around when his next target was killed, Larry might become a suspect. On the other hand, Larry's sudden disappearance might look suspicious to the cops. On the third hand, so far it appeared that everyone believed that Old Rick had died accidentally.

He decided that it would depend on his next target. If it was someone who might be a high risk target—someone whose lifestyle could result in some kind of accidental death—he would stay put for now. If it was someone he had to kill with a bullet or a garotte, he would disappear.

Having given himself permission to stay in the hotel, he went out for another great breakfast at the diner across the street.

Chapter 36

What could be better than having my client try to blackmail me? It was so over the top. I had to laugh. I really didn't think Mrs. Barnard would go to the trouble of making a false report about me, but these days, who knew?

It occurred to me to report Mrs. Barnard's threat to the firm's risk manager, but I'd had enough of my law partners. So I moved my lazy self from my cozy chair, and opened the front door to grab the paper. I could while away the day reading the Inky and subliminally thinking about my next career move. By the way, the Inky is the Philadelphia Inquirer. A fine paper.

And right there on the front page, but below the fold, was a short piece about the death of Richard Kozak, Senior, founder of We Love Trash. The police detective quoted in the article called his death a horrible accident. "He was known to sometimes drink a little too much," the detective said. Nicely put. Apparently, the guard at the Barnards' factory across the street had seen the lights go on briefly at the transfer station, and had called the old guy's son, who found the old man mashed to death. The police thought he had fallen in after activating the mechanism. That sounded strange to me, but then I wasn't there and I certainly was not a detective.

When my phone rang, I felt my gut tighten. So far, the phone had not delivered anything remotely resembling good news. It was Monica. Perhaps my luck was changing.

"Hello, darling," I said. "How nice to hear from you."

"I hope you still think so after I say what I have to say," she said.

"Oh, no," I said. "Is this about the guy who died over at the transfer station?"

"Sort of," she said. "Your client Mrs. Barnard is coming to see me today to talk about acquiring the property."

"She's not my client any more," I said.

"She made it sound as though she is," she said.

I sighed. I couldn't help it.

"I'd better write her a letter making clear that she's fired," I said.

Monica laughed.

"You rarely fire your clients."

"This is just the beginning. I'm getting out of the practice of law. It makes me want to tear my hair out."

There was a moment of silence while, I knew, Monica was refraining from mentioning my thinning hair.

"I thought you might want to give the Barnards a heads up about what she'll have to spend on environmental cleanup."

"Didn't you tell me that purchasers of contaminated property in an enterprise zone only have to delineate the pollution, not clean it up?"

"I did tell you that," said Monica. "But we're considering making this a federal site, and if we do, the cleanup will be costly."

"Monica, I'm out of the law biz. When you see Mrs. Barnard, you can tell her the good news."

"Okay, no problem," she said. She sounded quite cheerful.

We kissed on the phone, and said goodbye.

I laughed to myself about the dashing of Mrs. Barnard's plan for expansion. Best laid plans!

I should have remembered that the old bat had many tricks up her sleeve.

Chapter 37

As Larry Evans was wiping the last bit of egg off his face, his cell phone rang. He decided to let it ring until he exited the diner. He stuck it in his jacket pocket, got up and walked to the cashier. His phone rang, and stopped, rang and stopped.

"You know your phone is ringing?" the cashier said.

"Yes, ma'am," he said.

He paid his bill, walked out onto the sidewalk, and headed for Rittenhouse Square. He pulled the phone from his pocket, and answered it the next time it rang.

"Where are you now?" his handler said.

"Walking," Evans said.

"Did you leave the hotel, or are you still staying there?"

"I'm still there."

"Well, it won't matter after today, assuming you can finish your work that fast. I'm sending a photo of the guy you're after, and a little bit about him so you know what you have to work with. I'm sending it to your phone."

"Okay."

"The client is willing to pay double for this. I explained your concern about too many people dying."

"Fine," Evans said.

"Wow, I thought I'd hear a little more enthusiasm."

"Money is nice," Evans said. Then he hung up.

It was a cool morning, and he strolled into the Square over to a bench. He could smell earth as he sat down. It was nice to have some green around him. Not as nice as his own spread, but a good substitute considering he was in a city.

He checked his email. It made him laugh when he saw the most recent email address his handler had adopted: Life Partner. Attached to the email was a photo of a man that looked a lot like a wild boar. The email contained his name and a description of him.

Stanley Barnard. In a court battle with his elderly mother. Recently hospitalized for an adverse reaction to an ED drug. That made a light bulb go off in his head. Here was a guy who was clearly a pig. Evans should be able to poison him in food or drink. And his use of ED drugs was just the thing to provide a cover.

Larry now got to do something he actually enjoyed: tail someone. He loved the challenge of not being seen. He'd pick up the pig's trail outside of his office, follow him, and get it over with. Then he'd be back home by the end of the week. It was time. He was not really a city kind of person.

Chapter 38

Mrs. Barnard was a stubborn old lady, and her son Stanley was an annoying jerk. Shortly after she called to try to blackmail me, he did the same. Obviously, my home phone number was no longer private.

"Jack," he said when I answered the phone. "You've got to help me beat my mother in court."

"Stanley, there is nothing I can testify to that would help you, or for that matter your mother, in court."

"You can explain to the court that I've been running the business for years," he said. "That can help me."

"It doesn't help you on the question at the center of your lawsuit against your mother—who owns the business."

"Jack, I need your help."

Stanley's conversation was getting repetitive. And boring.

"Sorry, Stanley."

"You know," he said, "I'm thinking of suing you and your firm for fraud."

"What?"

"I was reading about a lawsuit some company brought against its lawyer for charging too much. That sounds like I have a good claim, doesn't it? Especially if I add a claim for malpractice."

If I were a cartoon character, smoke would be coming out of my ears right about now. I felt myself grinding my teeth, and made myself stop. Who knows if Stanley would make good on his threat? It seemed way over the top, even for him. Of course, he did have his mother's genes.

"You know what, Stanley?" I said.

"You've changed your mind?" he said.

"No. You do whatever you have to do. I can't help you." And then I hung up.

The two phone calls had effectively ended my leisurely coffee klatch with myself. I decided to head to the office and begin the task of dismantling my practice and my office.

My secretary and my clients would be minimally upset. They all liked me, but they were all realists. As for my clients, I could recommend some replacements for me, but they of course could choose any lawyer they wanted to.

I dressed in jeans and a t-shirt, and headed to my office downtown. The guard at the building entrance did a double take when he saw me.

"Is it Saturday?" he said.

"Only in my head," I said. I headed to the elevator bank.

As a door opened on an elevator, Marion came rushing out, stopped when she saw me, and stopped dead, causing a few exiting riders to trip over the back of her shoes.

"What's going on?" I said.

She gave me a look, took my arm, and moved me out of the path of the elevator doors.

"Shouldn't I be asking you that question?" she said.

"Have you been eating secretarial snoop?" I said.

"It's all over the office. They're kicking you out. What the heck is going on?"

I tried to decide whether the truth was better than a politic answer, but she beat me to it.

"Two-face again," she said. "Isn't it?"

I nodded.

"You know they're already calling your clients. They insisted on getting a list of clients with phone numbers from me this morning. I had to leave for a walk around the block. Don't you want me to come with you wherever you're going?"

I smiled at her.

"I have no idea where I'm going, or if I'm going anywhere, but I'll keep you in mind."

She leaned closer.

"Jack, can they just make you leave, without a partner vote?"

"How do you know there wasn't a partner vote?"

She looked affronted.

"You know the staff knows everything," she said.

I nodded.

"I think it's fair to say that what they're trying to do is a breach of our partnership agreement. But I don't really care."

"Oh, good," she said. "Fighting raises the blood pressure. I don't want anything to happen to you."

"Thank you, Marion. I'm touched."

"You're a good boss, for a lawyer," she said. She gave me a quick hug.

I entered an elevator as Two-face's secretary exited. She gave me a look that made me think she had seen Marion hug me. Poor Marion. I hoped she wouldn't be ousted because of her association with me.

Chapter 39

Larry Evans watched the pig for two days. He now knew that Stanley Barnard loved cocaine, that he favored using his car for his hits, and that he liked to dine at a small crab restaurant near his office. The restaurant had no bar, making a chance meeting almost impossible. Larry thought about spiking his coke, but that would only work if the pig bought into Larry being a coke dealer.

The third day of watching Stanley snuffle up powder on a small mirror in his car made Larry happy. He knew what he was going to do. He knew Stanley kept the mirror on his front seat, to make sure it was always within easy reach. Larry could sprinkle a little fairy dust on the mirror, which Stanley wouldn't notice in his voracious quest for a jolt. All Larry had to do was break into the car.

The pig finished his snuffling, and opened the car door. Stanley heaved his big body out of the car, huffing and puffing as he did so. He closed the car door, pausing with his hands on the car roof while he caught his breath. Then he headed for the restaurant. As he approached the front door, he turned toward his car, looking blankly at it. With a small shrug, he continued on into the restaurant.

Larry was dumbstruck. Stanley had forgotten to lock his car. How easy was this going to be? He almost laughed out loud. He reached into his inside pocket for the small clear vial that was waiting for him, and stared at the brown powder inside. He knew it wouldn't take much of the stuff.

Larry walked nonchalantly toward Stanley's car, toward the passenger door. He checked for possible watchers, but everyone seemed to be going about their business. He was pretty invisible. He crouched down beside the front passenger door, and slowly opened it. Holding his breath, he uncorked the vial and sprinkled a tiny amount of the brown powder on the mirror sitting on the front seat. He closed the door slowly, careful not to slam it. He recorked the vial, let out the breath he was holding, and put the vial back in his pocket. He waited until he had turned and walked ten paces before allowing himself to inhale.

Sometimes, life threw softballs, he thought. Now all he had to do was wait.

Chapter 40

When I got to my office, I had a surprise. Both good and bad news. I didn't have to pack up. Boxes lined the hallway. Someone else had taken it upon themselves to pack for me. David Smith, no doubt.

"And lo, he comes," I said.

Smith emerged from my office, holding a golf club. For a moment, I thought he was going to use it on me as a weapon.

"What the hell is this?" he said.

"A golf club," I said.

"A golf club with the firm's name on it," he said.

"Your point?"

"You stole this," he said.

"You're an idiot," I said. "The firm gave every partner a driver a few years back during our retreat. Meant to be inspiring, I think. You know, have drive? Be a driver of the firm?"

He looked at me with narrowed eyes.

"I haven't seen this in any one else's office," he said.

"Perhaps all my partners took their clubs home," I said. "Or gave them to charity."

"I'm confiscating this," he said.

I moved close to him.

"You know what, Dave? You're not."

I grabbed it.

"And the fact that two-face has a hard-on for me doesn't give you the right to act like an asshole. Just saying."

I turned and walked away with my driver in my hand. It seemed like a good time to see Ron.

I walked purposefully into his office, holding the club like…well, a club.

"What the hell!" he said.

Each eye looked alarmed.

"I don't want to hear bullshit from the staff," I said. "I'm still a partner here, and I can make your life a living hell if I take this firm to court. Because I don't care if I never work in this town again, and I'll have my money and your head at the same time."

I turned around and walked out. Just before I left, I noted that Ron had his mouth open. It apparently wasn't because he wanted to say something. It was because he was stunned.

I turned back to him.

"Ron, please tell David Smith to send all the items he's boxed up to my house. Paid for by the firm, of course."

Ron nodded.

I turned again, and left his office. I stood in the hall, club in hand, as several firm staff gave me a wide berth. I breathed deeply, smiled broadly and lowered the club.

"My work here is done," I said.

Holding the club loosely in my hand, and beginning to feel very lighthearted, I walked to the elevator, pressed the "down" button, and waited, humming, for the doors to open. When they did, I walked in, pressed the lobby button, and broke out into song. I think it was "I'm Going to Wash That Man Right Out of My Hair." There was one other occupant of the elevator, and he looked startled and then baffled, but by the time we reached the lobby, he was smiling. Happiness is infectious.

I never went back.

Chapter 41

Larry Evans decided not to wait to see the results of his handiwork. He knew Stanley Barnard would soon use his mirror to inhale some coke. He also knew that Stanley would not survive inhaling the powder he had sprinkled on the mirror. It was only a matter of time. He would go back to his hotel room, and wait for word from his handler.

He was feeling pretty good about this job. He'd managed without renting a car, using buses and taxis and his feet. He hated leaving any more of a trail than he had to. He could wipe down the hotel room before he left, pay for his room with his fake credit card, and disappear as Larry Evans.

He walked to the bus terminal, and got on the bus loading up for Center City Philadelphia. As before, some young urban cowboys with guitar cases and boots helped him blend in. He felt himself relaxing.

"I must be getting old," he said to himself. Usually, he couldn't relax until he was well away from a job, at home, when he was sure there was no blowback. It usually took about a week to unwind. He sat in the back of the bus, stretched his feet out in front of him, and closed his eyes. Maybe it was time for him to retire. He had enough money to do it. He didn't need to work.

"Jesus," he said.

The people around him on the bus looked at him, and he realized he had said it out loud. But he smiled at them, and they all settled down.

What had provoked his outburst was the realization that he was truly showing his colors as a baby boomer. Time to retire! Even for an assassin with no Social Security or Medicare. It made him smile all the way to the hotel.

Chapter 42

At this point in my life, the one person I wanted to share my happiness with was my daughter. In fact, I doubt that she remembered ever seeing me this happy and relaxed.

I was still carrying a golf club. No one seemed to notice, even though I had slung it over my shoulder. I guess I didn't look threatening. I thought I'd mosey over to Monica's office and see if she was available for a cup of coffee.

The club made it impossible, though, unless I was willing to check it at the desk. Monica worked for a government agency that was, of course, located in a government building, and no federal peace officer was going to allow me to carry a loaded golf club into the federal government.

"I'm sorry sir," the guard said, "but I can't let you take that into the building. We can hold it here at the desk for you."

I opened my mouth to protest, or at least say something snotty. Then I realized that without the club as a prop, I might not seem so jaunty. Did I want to de-jaunt myself?

Then I started laughing. The guard looked at me very seriously. Perhaps he thought I was a madman come to club the environmental protectors of the government like baby seals. But I was laughing at myself, for many reasons. One of those reasons is that in Philadelphia, if you are a native, the word for a "thing" is "jawn." As in "pass me that jawn, wudja?" Other cities might have different words for it, like "thingy" or "doodgie," but in Philadelphia, it was "jawn." And was I going to allow the guard to "de-jawn" me?

Maybe I was losing my marbles.

My cell phone started to ring and vibrate. I took myself out of line to enter the building, pulled my phone from my pocket, and looked at the screen. I didn't recognize the number, but I recognized the prefix. It was a Philadelphia municipal caller.

"Hello," I said.

"Jack," a woman said.

"Mrs. Barnard?"

What was she doing calling from a municipal office?

"Jack, it's Stanley. He's dead."

"What? Where are you? Are you okay?"

"I'm at police headquarters. The commissioner was nice enough to fetch me here. But I wanted to call you. You've been our lawyer for so long…"

She let her voice trail off. I recognized the role she was playing, since I had seen her do it over the years: great lady, highly educated, very refined. Not, in fact, much like the real woman on the other end of the phone.

I was trying to figure out how to express condolences and to tell Mrs. Bernard never to call me again when a male voice replaced hers on the phone.

"Jack Morgenthau," he said. "Seems like old times."

He obviously thought I should recognize his voice. I didn't. Before I could say anything, he enlightened me.

"It's Dolph, Dolph Rudy."

"Dolph! My god, how long has it been?"

"Probably since high school," he said. "Too many years ago to count."

"What's going on?" I said.

"It appears Stanley Barnard poisoned himself," he said.

"What?"

"Not on purpose," Dolph said. "No one would choose this particular way to die."

"What happened?"

He lowered his voice, presumably so Mrs. Barnard wouldn't catch what he had to say.

"The dickwad took Spanish fly to help him get it up. Too much—which is pretty much any at all—is fatal."

"It wasn't a pretty sight," Dolph said. He spoke even more quietly. "He ran into a local restaurant, with his hands around his own throat. He put his head in the men's room toilet."

"What?"

"He tried to drink the water in the bowl. We found him passed out with his head in the bowl."

The image was hard to take.

I remembered visiting Stanley in the hospital after he'd tried some erectile dysfunction drug and had some kind of heart problems. Did he think Spanish fly was more "natural"? Who could explain the inner thoughts of a randy, obese asshole?

As I thought the word "asshole," I looked up to notice that several people, including the guard, were staring at me. I still had the golf club over my shoulder, and I was staring into nothingness as I was gripping my phone. I turned away from the gapers.

"Why are you calling me, Dolph?"

"Mrs. Barnard believed it was necessary to discuss this with you."

"Why?"

"She told me about the business disputes between her and her son, and she said they had caused you to stop representing her. And now she wants you back."

"Is she a suspect? I mean, why call a lawyer?"

Dolph made some sort of snort into the phone.

"All I can tell you, Jack, is that the commissioner wanted me to treat her well. And no, she's not a suspect."

I had already decided that I was not a lawyer any more, and the thought of representing Mrs. Barnard for any reason didn't make me change my mind. To be polite, I asked Dolph to tell her that I would call her soon. Then I hung up before anyone could say another word.

I was stunned. Stanley was dead, poisoned in a most bizarre way. It didn't seem like an accident. It didn't feel right to me. Abandoning my quest for coffee with my daughter, I headed for home and my computer.

Chapter 43

Larry Evans was packing his clothes and his tools when the phone in the room rang. He eyed it with distaste. His contact should be calling his cell phone.

He picked up the handset.

"Yes?" he said.

"Oh, Mr. Evans, we see from your TV checkout that you're leaving us," a female voice said. "Is there anything we can help you with before you go? Was everything to your satisfaction?"

"No and yes," he said. He hung up.

His cell phone buzzed. Most likely, this call he was expecting.

"What?" he said.

"I wish I could get you to answer like a normal human being," his contact said.

"But I'm not," Larry Evans said. "So I don't."

His contact was silent. This was one of those times that he couldn't decide whether or not to bait Larry. He chose not to.

"I hope you haven't left yet," his contact said.

"I'm on my way out."

"I need you for one more job."

"Now you listen to me," Larry Evans said. "It's my life on the line, not yours. This is getting ridiculous. Two people involved in a business deal die, and if another one goes down, the cops are bound to put it together."

"Yeah, but here's the good part," said his contact. "The two dead guys were on different sides of the deal. So far it's just bad luck. The deal can still go ahead."

Larry Evans felt a bad feeling in his gut. He hated to leave before finishing the job, but he also hated to get caught. And this felt like tempting some kind of fate.

"You never told me that there would be three jobs here," he said.

"I'm looking out for you, man," his contact said. "Didn't I get you more money for the second hit?"

Larry Evans did some quick calculations, and thought about his almost-decision to retire.

"Double what I got for the fat guy," he said. "Maybe I'll do the third. But that's it, not just for Philly, for good."

"What? You're at the top of your game. Why would you quit now?"

"I'm changing hotels," he said. "Call my cell in a few hours."

He hung up. Was he crazy to do this? Probably. But the temptation of all that cash was the hook. His retirement fund, in one quick deal.

He finished packing, and decided to walk a few blocks before taking a cab to his next hotel. He'd miss the great breakfast at the diner, but what the hell.

Chapter 44

I got home just as my phone was ringing. I hated when that happened. I decided to let my voicemail pick it up. It was undoubtedly my local pharmacy telling me my reflux medicine was ready for renewal and pickup.

I headed for my home office, then stopped in the hall. This would now be my only office. Not my home office. How lucky that I loved this office.

I sat at my desk with the view of the Delaware River through the window beside me. The same Delaware River that the transfer station was possibly polluting. I didn't really care. I watched the local sailing club setting up the course for their daily races. A tug pulled a barge. Another tug pushed a different barge. Some day I'd have to figure out why some barges were pulled and others pushed. In fact, soon I'd have plenty of time to pursue these and other important conundrums.

I fired up my computer. Unlike the old days of computing, when I would have to go and make a cup of coffee before the machine booted up, I was instantly online. I sat in my chair and stared at the screen. I typed "Stanley Barnard" in my search engine window.

Not surprisingly, it presented me with 200,000 mentions of Stanley within a millisecond. I added the word "died" to my search, and two of our local network TV stations' websites popped up, with brief stories on his accidental poisoning. Both reporters were circumspect about the poison, implying it was

Stanley's hope to use a "natural" substance instead of Viagra or Cialis for his sexual dysfunction. Neither actually voiced the words "Spanish fly."

I looked up Spanish fly. I discovered two things. First, it is readily available on the internet despite the fact that almost every website that discusses it describes it as highly toxic and usually fatal. It is sold legally to dermatologists to use as a blistering agent to remove warts.

Secondly, it is made from ground up beetles whose bodies contain large amounts of a chemical known as cantharidin, a poison so toxic that the homicidal Medicis used it to kill their enemies. If taken internally, it burns its victims from the inside out. There is no cure. Victims die within hours, writhing in horrible pain.

Poor Stanley. The image of him burning up inside, and the thought of the agony he went through... No one should die that way.

But did he really kill himself accidentally? The mention in the online literature of the Medicis set me thinking. They were a family of aristocrats jockeying for power and money. Catherine de Medici in particular was a micromanager of her sons' lives. Who did I know like that?

And yet, as ruthless as she was, I couldn't imagine Mrs. Barnard poisoning her son. Or certainly not in a way that would cause him such agony.

Then I started thinking about the other death associated with the real estate near there. The head of the family that owned the transfer station had died in a peculiar way. Were the deaths related?

Mrs. Barnard benefitted from the removal of the two impediments to her plan to expand. I didn't think she had the physical ability to throw someone into a garbage crusher. But she could have hired someone to do it.

I couldn't decide whether or not I was being paranoid, fanciful and otherwise ridiculous. Would Mrs. Barnard have killed her son and heir? Was it possible?

I thought some more, and then decided I should report this to the cops. And then I re-decided that I shouldn't. I felt as though somehow reporting Mrs. Barnard for my suspicions would entangle me in attorney-client privileged areas.

Even though I was glad to be out of the firm, I now missed one of its advantages—having someone to give me feedback and guidance, someone with whom to share my suspicions.

What a revolting situation. I needed something liquid to help me think. Coffee? Scotch? I looked at my watch. Both. Together. I got up to make it happen.

Once again the phone rang. This time, I glanced at the caller id. It said "blocked." Usually, that meant Monica calling. I answered the phone.

"Oh, Dad, thank heavens you picked up," Monica said.

"Why didn't you try my cell?" I said.

"I did," she said. "It went straight to voicemail."

I pulled my phone out of my pocket. No charge. Dead as a doornail.

"Sorry," I said. "Are you okay?"

"Yes and no," she said. She sounded as though she could cry.

"What's going on?"

"I'm being punished for lording it over you with my job," she said. She made a noise like a hiccup, as though she was laughing and crying at the same time.

I sat back down at my desk. I could tell this wasn't going to be a quick conversation.

I could hear Monica take a deep breath.

"Dad, I feel like a jerk and a liar and a cheat. My boss made me renege on a promise I made years ago to a defendant."

I waited. Since Monica was none of those things, something must have happened.

"I've been handling this superfund litigation on a site in Bucks County," she said. "It's been going on for years."

I know from her descriptions of these "litigations" that the cases never went to trial. Hundreds of defendants, sued by the government, took years to reach a settlement with the government and each other. A true private lawyer's dream— enough years of work to send your children through college.

"Okay," I said.

"I settled with Carbone Electric years ago. We have a settlement agreement. The company paid us $100,000. They didn't have to be part of the superfund lawsuit anymore. They were pretty happy."

"Okay."

"The company's lawyer and I have had a very cordial relationship. Up until now."

Now she had me confused. Was this personal or business related? I waited.

"Back when I negotiated the settlement with the company, I released the company from all claims for cleanup. We had a standard release that I sent to the company."

"Okay," I said.

"Their lawyer called me to say that the claim for natural resource damages should be explicitly included."

"What's that?"

"It's a payment of money to make up for the environmental damage to the ground or the air or the water that was polluted. It's like loss of use of the resource. Or to put it another way, to make up for the fact that the area will never be pristine again."

"Okay, I get it," I said.

"I went to my supervisor at the time, who told me that we couldn't change the language of our standard settlement agreement. But that I could assure the company that we hadn't sued for natural resource damages in any superfund case yet."

I began to see where this was going.

"I told the company they could relax. We didn't sue for natural resource damages."

"I guess the government has changed its position," I said.

"Yes, and I'm the one left holding the bag," she said. "I had to call the company lawyer and tell him we were going to sue Carbone Electric for NRD at the same site. He went ballistic. I would have, too, if

161

I'd been in his shoes. My reputation as a straight shooter is in shreds."

"Oh, jeez. Honey, I'm so sorry."

Monica's reputation for honesty was important to her, as it was to any lawyer. More to the point, the legal community in Philadelphia was a small one for such a large city, and word of her perfidy would spread quickly. I truly felt bad for her. And I knew there was no quick fix.

"Time heals all wounds," I said. Even to my ears, I sounded lame.

"You know, Dad, that sucks. It's like when I broke up with George and I was so upset and you said there are plenty of fish in the sea. Not what I want to hear."

I sighed.

"I wish I could tell you something more positive," I said. "You'll just have to wait until people forget this."

"But I can't say to people any more, trust me."

"You can trust your government," I said.

"What?"

"It won't come as a shock to people that the government isn't always trustworthy."

"Why are you not making me feel better?"

"I'm sorry. But, Monica, I do believe that this will diminish and disappear. People will forget. And you have to just keep explaining that there was a change in policy."

"I'm so angry, I'm shaking," she said. "And for the first time since high school, I'd like to kill someone."

I heard her begin to cry. I felt helpless. This wasn't a boo-boo I could stick a band-aid on. She had been shafted by a co-worker, in a way that was going to cause repercussions for her.

Unfortunately, that made two of us. Real life. Adulthood. Sometimes, it sucks.

Chapter 45

Larry Evans looked around the storefronts on Walnut Street. Most were high-end stores. He longed to be out of the city and on his farm. But if he had to live in a city, this one appealed to him. Not too big. Not too small. A little voice in his head said: Just right!

Where had that come from? It suffused him with an odd mix of feelings. He was overwhelmed with a wash of sadness.

Evans was not big on introspection. Rarely did anything bother him about himself. He was still angry, though, at his killing of the prostitute. It was unnecessary. He had been wounded to his core, and drunk, and that was a bad combination that led to mistakes. He had resolved not to let it happen again, and he knew he wouldn't. It didn't occur to him to wonder why he felt the way he felt.

But his budding interest in retirement puzzled him. What would he do with himself if he "retired?" Go to college? Then to medical school? The whole idea seemed absurd.

At the corner of Walnut Street and Sixteenth, a fruit vendor was offering sad-looking apples and pears. The smell of rotting fruit intensified as he got closer. There was a hint of peaches, and another wash of sadness hit him.

He didn't stop walking. No one looking at him would have thought he was going through any sort of crisis. His face was a poker player's. But he wondered about his usefulness to his partner, his clients, himself, if he suddenly started decompensating. He had never let feelings get to him before.

Maybe this was the right time to "retire."

He mentally shook himself. This was not a useful exercise. He had work to do. He sped up his pace, walking with purpose to the corner of Walnut and Broad. He flagged down a cab. He knew of a hotel that would have room for him even without a reservation, one that catered to airplane pilots and flight attendants. He would head there, get a room, and wait for his contact to call.

Chapter 46

The next ringing phone was my cell phone. I could see it was Mrs. Bernard. I would express my condolences and then beg off.

"Hello, Mrs. Barnard," I said. "I'm so sorry for your loss."

"Oh, Jack, every time someone answers the phone knowing it's me I get shocked all over again. I'm back in the dark ages in my mind, when the phone just rang. It didn't tell you who was calling."

She sounded old, suddenly. It made my suspicions about her ludicrous. She was an elderly, crotchety woman who had just lost her son. I could feel myself thawing toward her.

"I'm so sorry about Stanley," I said. "And I was so shocked when you called from City Hall, I didn't have a chance to tell you then."

"I know, Jack. I understand. And thank you for your condolences. Stanley was my only child, and even though we didn't always see eye to eye, I'll miss him. Thank heavens for my grandchildren. I'm hoping they'll come in and take over the company now that Stanley's gone."

I thought of Stanley's offspring. The oldest was twenty. Somewhat young to take over a huge operation.

"They're ready to do that?" I said. "Even at their tender ages?"

I heard her sigh.

"No, I guess not quite, although I was only 19 when I started this company. Kids mature later today then when I was growing up."

"I guess you'll have to hang in there a while longer," I said. Actually, I didn't say it. I thought it, though. Mrs. Bernard might not have had the equilibrium to laugh at her own mortality right now.

"Stanley's wife will come in and learn the business, and then the kids as they graduate college. Not exactly how I expected my legacy to continue, but at least it will continue."

"You've already talked to Stanley's wife?" I said.

"Of course. His death is a great sadness, but there's still a business to run."

I wondered if his wife and children were upset, but I didn't know how to broach it.

"How are Stanley's wife and kids taking this?" I said.

"Well, the kids are upset, I think."

That's all she said. I'd guess Stanley's wife wasn't too happy with his obsession with erections, particularly if she wasn't the intended target.

"Listen, Mrs. Barnard," I said, "I've resigned from my firm and I'm leaving the legal profession. I'm sorry about that, but I hope you'll understand that it's a personal decision and has nothing to do with my clients."

"Oh," she said.

I waited.

"Well, that's just too bad," she said.

I waited.

"I hope you don't mind if I continue to use your firm," she said. "And I'd like to be able to call you now and then to see how you're doing. And your daughter."

"My daughter?"

"Well, yes, I know you're close," she said.

I guess she wanted to keep tabs on Monica's work on the polluted transfer station across from Barnard Hardware. The old lady was certainly a piece of work.

"Well, Jack, I've got to go. Enjoy your retirement."

She hung up without waiting for me to say goodbye.

Chapter 47

The old lady hung up the phone and stared at it. She wasn't happy about Jack's departure from his law firm. She wanted to keep tabs on his daughter for the next few days, and on her plans for the transfer station across the street.

She had lived this long by not allowing herself to get distracted from her goals. Thinking about Jack was a distraction. She sat back in her chair, careful not to put her head back. She didn't want to flatten her wig in the back. It was a trick she had learned early in her life, even when the hairdo was her real hair. Although it was uncomfortable never to allow her head to touch a pillow, her personal code, always to look like a million bucks, required it. She had made do with the discomfort, using a neck rest in bed so her hair wouldn't be dislodged. Wearing a wig had obviated the need for that, and finally in her 90s she was getting a full night's restful sleep.

She closed her eyes. She couldn't decide how she felt about losing Stanley. On the one hand, he was her only child, the son on whom she had pinned her hopes for the company and her legacy. On the other hand, he had been a pig and a boor, and his vision for the company was short-sighted. She hoped she could mold her grandchildren into something better, something more like herself.

And she knew she didn't have much time. She felt well enough, but she wouldn't live forever. At her age, a year or two felt like the blink of an eye. It was time for her to continue working toward her goal.

She had to expand her business or contract it, and she couldn't bear the idea of going backwards. Barnard Hardware would expand, with or without Stanley.

She had set the wheels in motion, and could only wait, and plan, and play it by ear as events unfolded around her.

Chapter 48

What was I going to do with the rest of my life? After Mrs. Barnard hung up on me, my brain was in turmoil.

I was trained as a lawyer. I'd been a lawyer my entire working life. Since I didn't want to practice law, what else was there?

I was a good problem-solver. I could create solutions for people's problems. I could be what is now commonly called "a fixer." Not a political fixer, since I had virtually no political influence, and I didn't know anyone who did. Certainly not an enforcer, since I wasn't particularly strong and I doubted that anyone would find me intimidating. So what kind of fixer could I be? Who the hell knows? Maybe an idea would come to me in a flaming pie, as John Lennon used to say.

Or perhaps I could offer problem-solving advice, in a newspaper or online. My column or blog would be called "Ask Jack." "Dear Jack. How long can I keep a hard-boiled egg in the refrigerator? I can't remember when I cooked it. Eggsistential." "Dear Eggsistential. If you can't remember when you cooked it, it has been in your refrigerator too long."

I had to stop thinking about the future. Something would come along. I just had to be receptive to it. I know there is life after law.

I settled down in my den, and turned on the television. I flipped channels until I found what I wanted: back to back episodes of "Law and Order."

If you can't be part of the action, you can at least watch the action.

But I found my mind wandering. So many outrageous things happen in law firms, and I knew about quite a few of them. The internet had helped to popularize strange law firm shenanigans, but there were many that never made it to the web.

In our firm alone, we had enough neuroses to fill a diagnostic manual just for lawyers. We had the litigation partner who lost his nerve every time an actual trial came up, forcing someone else in the firm to try the case. We had the office manager whose affair with the firm's comptroller gave her unbelievable power over the firm's finances. We had the lawyer whose wife and child were killed in a car accident, and who took that life-altering moment to transform himself within months from a chubby, spectacled nonentity into a slender, contact-wearing powerhouse.

And then there were the Law and Order-ready deaths, ripped from the headlines—the flip-flop wearing partner who jumped to his death from a fire escape, the staff member whose husband murdered her and then killed himself.

And my point was, and I had a point, that I was not going to miss law firm idiocy.

Perhaps I could offer myself to firms as some kind of lay psychiatrist, to weed out the loonies. I thought back to when our firm had hired a psychologist to
figure out why so many lawyers were unhappy with management. Everyone was interviewed. We were supposed to speak honestly about our feelings about

the firm. We were not, however, guaranteed anonymity. We were damned no matter what we did. If we refused to speak in a meaningful and substantive way, the management committee said we weren't team players. If we honestly expressed ourselves, we were traitors. The psychologist rendered a report that said we were schizophrenic as a firm; we couldn't decide whether we wanted to be a good place to work or a very profitable business.

Needless to say, that experiment proved nothing. And nothing improved. Could I do better in another law firm? Probably not.

I turned my mind back to the television. I needed to empty my brain. I tried to let everything go except for what was marching in front of my eyes. I really loved "Law and Order." I was hoping for a marathon. I would sink into the sofa and turn my brain over to Dick Wolf for a while.

Chapter 49

Larry Evans checked into the hotel. The lobby was crawling with people in uniform. Pilots and flight attendants, all looking vaguely military, except for four Asian women kitted out in brightly colored sarongs. He certainly didn't fit in with the look of this crowd.

But no one paid any attention to him, which was what he wanted. He took the key card to his room, rode up in the elevator, and walked down a corridor smelling of cigarettes to his room. The room smelled of some unidentifiable floral bouquet. His view was over Delaware Avenue. He didn't care.

He put his case in the closet, next to the room safe. He sat on the desk chair, his cell phone out of his pocket and on the desk. He tried to decide if this would be his last job. What the hell else would he do with himself?

He looked at his phone. Ring, dammit. He wanted to get on with this work, get out of Philadelphia, and get back to his ranch and his cabin. He would relax and determine if he wanted to spend all his time there, riding big equipment.

It rang.

"Go," he said.

"What's with you?" his contact said. "I would have thought you'd be happy to talk to me since this is your last big job, right?"

Larry Evans sighed. There was a cosmic joke here, he was sure.

"Tell me about the job," he said.

"This will be a fitting end to your illustrious career," his contact said. "It's a pain in the ass government employee."

"Okay."

"You'll still be Larry Evans for this," his contact said. "She's been keeping tabs on the transfer station deal. She'll know who you are. Or at least she thinks she knows who you are."

"Okay."

"I figured you could use that to get to her. You know how they protect government employees. It's your opening."

"Got it," said Larry Evans.

"She's with the EPA. You know, the Environmental Protection Agency."

Evans sighed.

"I do read, occasionally. Plus I still remember the briefing book you sent me. I remember what the EPA is."

"Good. Her office is on Arch Street, not far from City Hall. Maybe you'll do the job and then hop a subway out of the city."

"Are you doing my job for me now?"

"Just saying."

"Me too," said Larry Evans. "I'll take care of it. I still have the book. I'll make a plan. You'll hear from me when it's done."

He hit the "end call" button.

The book was in his suitcase with his tools. He had planned to carry it home with him and burn it.

But for now, he opened his case and removed the book. He flipped through the pages until he found the EPA employee. A woman. That didn't bother him. Young. That didn't bother him. The fact that she worked in a guarded federal government building bothered him. He had to plan this carefully.

Larry Evans memorized the face in the photo: Monica Morgenthau. He might be spending some time tailing her from Arch Street, following her home. He couldn't really imagine how he could get into her building without detection, or, more importantly, how he could kill her in the building and then get out without detection.

He fell back onto the hotel bed and closed his eyes, determined to formulate a plan. Without intending to, he fell asleep.

Chapter 50

I awoke with a start, my neck aching from my position on the sofa. The Law and Order marathon was still marching across the TV screen. I heard the house phone ringing. I fumbled for it, banging the receiver several times on the table by accident.

"Hello," I said.

"Jack, you okay?"

I was still shaking cobwebs out of my head, but I recognized the voice: my brother Steve.

"Yes, I'm fine. Just waking up from a nap."

"I called your office. They told me you quit."

"That's sort of true," I said.

"You needed a nap so bad you quit your job?"

My brother, the comedian.

"You know I haven't been enjoying myself there," I said.

"I know. Anything I can do?"

My brother Steve is also a lawyer. He has his own boutique law firm. He's the only partner. He often says the only partner disputes he has are when he looks in the mirror.

"I think I need to take some time off," I said. "But thanks."

"I have an extra office if you want to park there, permanently or temporarily."

"Thanks, Steve."

"Well..."

"I'm fine," I said. "Really. We'll talk in a few days."

"If you're sure," he said.

"I'm sure."

We hung up. Although Steve is my baby brother, he often thinks he's my mother. Which is often very nice.

I thought briefly about continuing to practice on my own, or with Steve. But really, I had no desire to be a lawyer any more. I didn't like my clients. What if I started to have disagreements with my brother? There was no way this was going to work for me.

I turned off the TV and walked to my computer. Old habits die hard, and I wanted to read my emails. Just to see if there was anything interesting.

There was something interesting, buried among the emails excoriating me for being such a bad partner and the others congratulating me on getting out of the firm in one piece. The interesting email was from my old law school friend Jimmy Duffy, who now lives in London and works at one of the huge law conglomerates.

"Hey, Jackie," it said. He was the only living person allowed to call me that. "Long time, I know. I have a favor to ask, but it's for a paying client. Which means it's a paying favor."

Apparently, one of his firm's clients was looking for his daughter, whom he hadn't seen in ten years. He thought she was probably in the U.S. Could I find her, or hire a private investigator to find her?

Now that seemed like an interesting challenge. Could I be a finder of people? In my youth, I had tracked down witnesses for the senior partners in the litigation department. How hard could it be? Jimmy might be doing me a favor instead of getting one from me.

I felt a burst of adrenaline. I felt a spurt of excitement. I stopped being pissed off for the moment. And I wrote Jimmy back, saying I'd be happy to take the assignment.

Jack Morgenthau, finder of missing persons!

Chapter 51

The vibrating cell phone in his pocket awakened him. He looked at his watch in disbelief. He'd slept for over an hour, and he felt disoriented. The sound of the phone hadn't penetrated his sleeping mind.

He ignored the phone and walked into the bathroom, turned on the faucet and splashed cold water on his face. He sucked some into his mouth and spat. What an awful feeling. He wouldn't answer his phone until he was fully awake.

His phone rang and vibrated several more times before he decided to answer it.

"What?" he said.

"Why didn't you answer your phone?" his handler said.

"What do you want?" he said.

"Our client called with an offer to make your job a little easier."

"Now what?"

"She wants to set up a meeting with the EPA girl and you and her to act as though the deal, with you as an investor, is going to happen. It gives you an in with the girl."

Larry Evans was silent. He had to admit, it could make his assignment easier to have immediate access to the girl. On the other hand, he didn't like having another human being, particularly a client, at the introductory meeting. He much preferred to remain anonymous to those who hired him.

"I know how you feel about having your clients on hand when you work," his handler said. "But this one says she knows you already. She saw you leaving the transfer station the night you killed the old man."

Larry Evans felt his heart start beating faster. Had she been following him? How could she have seen him? He thought back to that night, the darkness and the silence. It wasn't possible.

"It's not possible," he said.

"I'm telling you, she described you pretty accurately."

"This is not good," he said.

"You're telling me? Your best qualification for your job is that no one ever sees you."

Larry Evans had a feeling of dread. He hadn't had that feeling for so long that he wasn't sure what it was. Was he having a heart attack?

"Just a minute," he said.

He put his phone down, took his own pulse. He didn't think he was having a heart attack. He picked up his cell.

"Go ahead," he said.

"You're acting really strange, man. Are you up for this job?"

"I'm fine," Larry Evans said.

He listened with half his brain to the meeting set up. With the other half of his brain, he tried to think how anyone could have seen him that night at the transfer station. Someone with some kind of night vision paraphernalia could have, he supposed. It worried him that he could have been seen. And it worried him that he didn't realize it. Usually, his sixth sense told him if there was someone around. His "lizard brain." If it was failing him now, it probably was time to hang it up.

Chapter 52

I called Jimmy's client. It turned out he was already in the States, looking for his daughter. He was in New York City, staying at a high end hotel in the theater district. Even beyond the upper class British accent, he sounded educated. This deflated me somewhat. He had probably already tried the usual methods of finding her that I stupidly thought would be my ticket to success—web searches, both for free and for money.

His name was Charles Graybolt. ("Call me Charles," he said.) His daughter had been missing for a bit over ten years. She was 28, and she had left home at 18 after a terrible fight with her father.

"I do feel it was my fault she left," said Charles. "I'd like to apologize, and see if she is willing to be my daughter again."

"What was the fight about? How was it your fault? Why did you wait ten years to find her?"

"That's certainly a lot of questions at once," said Charles.

"Please feel free to answer them one at a time," I said.

I hadn't meant to browbeat the man, but something about the situation didn't seem right to me. Maybe his daughter had kept herself hidden for good reasons.

There was a pause after I responded to him. I might already have pissed off my first client as a people finder.

He blew into the phone, which I didn't take personally. It was as though he'd been holding his breath.

"Her name is Charlotte," he said. "My only child."

I was impressed. The man had managed to answer a question I hadn't even asked.

"We fought about her mother," he said. "I was divorced from her mother."

I waited, but Charles said no more.

"What was the fight about?" I said.

"Charlotte believed that I hadn't treated her mother right."

One of the things I learned over my years as a lawyer is that clients will lie to you for many different reasons. I can't stop them from doing it, but I can try to get the truth out of them.

"What does Charlotte believe about you now?"

"I don't know," he said.

"What was it Charlotte thought was wrong about how you treated your former wife?"

There was a much longer pause.

"Charlotte thought I murdered her mother," Charles said.

That took my breath away.

"You English and your understatement," I said. "Certainly, murdering someone is the height of not treating someone right."

"Yes, well…" Charles said. "It's not something I like to talk about. I'm telling you because you pressed me, and because Jimmy told me to be candid with you."

"Did you murder your wife?"

"Of course not!"

"How did she die?"

"She died just recently," he said. "She died in a mental institution that had been her home for years."

At this point, my head was spinning. My conversation with Charles reminded me of a trial advocacy course I'd taken in law school, where I was required to find out a witness's vocation. The witness was impossible to pin down. He kept saying he was "in the protection business." I finally got him to admit he was an insurance agent.

"Charles," I said. "Do you really want to find your daughter?"

"Why yes, of course," he said. "Why do you ask?"

"Because you're making this hard. What's going on?"

"My wife, when she was my wife, was deranged. I don't say that lightly. I don't say that meanly. She was very ill, and she had to be hospitalized. It appeared unlikely that she could ever recover. So I told Charlotte that she had died in the hospital. And I got my divorce quietly. She never knew her mother was still alive."

"Why did she think you murdered her mother?"

"When I remarried, I married her mother's best friend. Charlotte thought I'd murdered her mother to marry my current wife."

"For heaven's sake," I said.

I felt exasperated.

"Why didn't you just tell Charlotte the truth at that point?" I said.

"It seemed rather complicated," he said. "I'd have to admit to her that her mother was still alive, and that I wasn't letting her see her mother for good reasons."

"What good reasons?" I said.

"Her mother tried to kill her. Several times."

"What? How?"

"She fed her poison. She tried to drown her in the bathtub. That sort of thing."

That sort of thing?

"You have to understand," Charles said. "This was a long time ago. Her mother was incarcerated almost immediately after I found out what was happening. Neither of them has seen each other for a long time."

I decided that, like every client I'd ever had, Charles was editing his story to appear in a favorable light. And as with every other client, I had to independently verify what he was telling me. For all I knew, Charles was a serial killer trying to find his daughter in order to murder her. I would call Jimmy in the morning to find out what he knew about his client.

"Why now, Charles? What made you decide to look for her after all these years?"

"Charlotte's mother has died. And she left a large amount of money to Charlotte. I thought she should know. I thought she should have the money."

"Where do you think she is?" I said. "Why do you think she's in the United States?"

"A friend of mine was convinced he saw her in Philadelphia."

"Who is the friend?"

"My best friend from the time I was a boy. Upton Montclair. He was teaching at one of your universities for a year, but he's back in the UK. I can give you his number if you like."

"Yes, I'd like," I said.

This new profession was shaping up to be almost as frustrating as practicing law. Clients—can't live with them, can't live without them.

Chapter 53

The old lady offered to meet with the so-called Larry Evans and Monica Morgenthau at Barnard Hardware's headquarters. She invited one of the owners of the transfer station to the meeting. The first time should be on the up and up. Maybe, she thought, it would be a good idea to invite Jack Morgenthau, too. Actually, it was a great idea. No guarantee he'd come, of course, but she could try.

Her daughter-in-law was down the hall at her son's desk, trying to come to grips with the job. She would be fine. And the business would thrive, and her grandchildren would carry on her legacy.

The old lady didn't want to die, but it gave her pleasure to daydream about what would happen afterward, after she was dead. Even though she wouldn't be around to see it, she was setting it all in motion, and imagining the outcome was pleasing to her. Her life had always been her business. It was her life's dream for Bernard Hardware to prosper. For Stanley to carry on the great experiment she had launched.

Oh, Stanley. She remembered how cute he was as a baby. His pudgy little arms circling her legs as she strode out to the office, laughing as he wept, picking him up and putting him in the sitter's arms. He was a beautiful baby, everybody said so.

If Stanley hadn't been such a pig, such a jerk, such a disappointment…

However, as her grandson said, it is what it is. Stanley was what he was. Not what his mother wanted him to be.

She felt a little sorry, intellectually, that Jack Morgenthau would soon lose his daughter. Monica had done him proud. She hoped he had soaked up the wonderfulness, since it would have to last him for the rest of his life.

She sat up in her chair with a start. She was beginning to be senile. She wasn't thinking clearly. The owners of the transfer station would know Larry Evans and wonder why he had just disappeared after Old Rick's death. She couldn't ask them to a meeting. She would leave it to Larry Evans to figure out how to remove Monica. She'd make the introductions, then leave. She could rely on a professional not to make a mess in her office.

She admired Larry Evans. He did his work with finesse. She would give him carte blanche on how to handle it.

One more week, she thought, and she would be a completely happy woman.

Chapter 54

I was really torn about finding Charlotte Graybolt. I was imagining how I would feel if I'd been estranged from my daughter, and had the chance to make it right. But I was worried that Charles Graybolt was some kind of pervert who would harm his daughter.

I called my friend Jimmy in London. I was so focused on tracking down the origins of the Graybolt mess that I forgot about the time difference. Jimmy reminded me.

"Hullo," he said. His voice sounded muffled.

"Jimmy," I said.

"Bloody hell, Jack," he said. "It's three a.m."

I apologized profusely, and offered to call him back at a more reasonable hour.

"I'm awake now," he said. "What is it?"

"Charles Graybolt," I said.

"Yes?"

"Is he a serial killer pervert who wants to off his daughter?"

I heard Jimmy exhale.

"You cannot believe that I would saddle you with someone like that," he said.

"But how well do you know him?"

"He's been my client for years. Never killed anyone. Never raped anyone. Can I go back to sleep?"

"Yes, of course," I said. And again abased myself for waking him.

So Jimmy allayed my anxiety, somewhat. Maybe the dad was a do-gooder, and just wanted his daughter to inherit her mother's money. But even a long-time client could fool you, and be a monster. I knew that from watching Law and Order.

My next step was to talk to Upton Montclair, Charles Graybolt's friend. Mindful of the mistake I made with Jimmy, I refrained from calling him. If he was back in the UK, as Charles had told me, it would also be three a.m. for him.

I added calling him to my to-do list for the next morning. I paced around my home for awhile, and then called Monica.

"Hi, Dad," she said. She sounded pleased to hear from me.

"Want to go out to dinner?" I said.

"Sure, sounds great," she said. "It might have to be on the late side. Believe it or not, I'm going to a meeting at Barnard Hardware this afternoon."

"No kidding. How come?"

"Mrs. Barnard wants to discuss the environmental issues on the property across the street. She says she has an interest in acquiring it. Since she's in her 90s, I agreed to go to her place."

"That was nice of you," I said. "Just be careful around her. She's a witch."

"Oh, Dad," she said. "What is she going to do, shoot me? I could blow her over in a nanosecond."

"Well, if you can give me a rough estimate of when you think you'll be done, I could meet you in the neighborhood. There's that great crab shack-y kind of place nearby."

"Great! You know I love dives like that. How about if we meet there at seven?"

"Sounds good," I said.

I found myself smiling. I was really looking forward to having another opportunity to see my wonderful daughter.

Chapter 55

Larry Evans was extremely jumpy about two things. One was the fact that the old lady supposedly knew what he looked like. The other was that he was heading back to the very same street block on which he had killed Old Rick. He thought he was probably making the mistake of his career continuing with this job. But he had never bailed out on a job, and he couldn't imagine doing it now.

Of course, he couldn't remember having felt this bad before a job, or this jittery. The one time he had been nervous was after he had garotted a soldier at Fort Dix; he was afraid he wouldn't have time to get the hell out of there before the MPs found him. But that had worked out just fine.

He was driving a rental car. Better to use different methods of transportation each time he came to this neighborhood. It had a GPS unit, but he didn't use it, didn't even turn it on. He unplugged it from the car battery. He used his handy pocket knife to pry off the back of the unit, and he removed the rechargeable battery. He didn't want anyone tracing his movements.

He saw the Barnard Hardware sign coming up on his right, and slowed to a crawl. There was a white Cadillac sitting in the empty parking lot. As he parked his rental next to the Caddy, a cab pulled into the lot close behind him. A woman stepped out, leaned in to the taxi, paid her fare and got a receipt. When she stood up and turned toward him, he saw it was his quarry. Monica Morgenthau. Pretty young girl. Too bad she wouldn't have time to pass her genes on to a child.

He stepped out of the rental, and held up his right hand in greeting.

"I'm Larry," he said. He smiled. Mr. Charm returns.

Chapter 56

I received an email from Upton Montclair, telling me he was awake and could he call me? I emailed back yes.

A moment later my home phone rang.

"Mr. Morgenthau?" he said.

"Yes, Mr. Montclair," I said. "Please call me Jack."

"You Americans!" he said. He didn't reciprocate.

"Charles Graybolt asked me to call you," he said. "About Charlotte."

"Yes," I said. I said it in a way I thought was encouraging.

"I spent this past year in your lovely city as a visiting professor," he said. "At Drexel University."

"I believe Charles told me that," I said.

"As my wife and I were packing up our things, it must be about three weeks ago now, we decided to take a break and walk around the University of Pennsylvania campus. That's when I saw Charlotte. Sitting on a bench, eating a sandwich."

"How did you know it was Charlotte?" I said.

"Her father and I have been close friends for years. I've known Charlotte since she was born. Her looks are unmistakable. A very pretty girl. And her looks haven't changed a bit."

"Did you talk to her?" I said.

"I waved, and my wife and I began to walk toward her, but she either pretended she didn't see us or she really didn't see us. She left the bench, went behind some arbor vitae and disappeared."

"Did you see her again?"

"No. My wife and I hurried after her, but we didn't see her again. Very odd, I'd say."

"You're sure she would know who you are?"

"Of course! Charles and I have been friends for donkey's years. Apart from having less hair than I used to, I look the same as I did when Charlotte left."

I thanked Montclair for calling me, and asked him to let me know if there was anything he had forgotten to tell me.

I was beginning to feel like a private investigator. Then I had an uncomfortable thought. I needed a license to practice law. Did I need a license to privately investigate? To locate a missing person?

Then my mind veered into the tender area of whether my client was lying about anything (of course he was), and if so, what. When his daughter first left home, did Charles ever report his daughter missing to the police in England? Had he tried to find her before?

Suddenly, I felt like a fraud. I worried that Charles was somehow playing me. Why is nothing ever easy?

But there was a redeeming aspect to Montclair's conversation with me. If he and his wife saw Charlotte on the Penn campus, maybe she was a student there, or perhaps she worked there. I had a close friend who was in the Office of General Counsel, and I thought she would probably be willing to help me determine if Charlotte Graybolt was affiliated with Penn. Of course, it wouldn't help if Charlotte was calling herself something else, or if she worked nearby and just decided to eat lunch on the campus.

So I looked in my contacts for Barbara DuQuesne, assistant general counsel, and gave her a call. It was worth the old college try, wasn't it?

Chapter 57

Larry Evans tried to block out the aroma wafting from the transfer station across the street. Since he was playing the educated investor, it wouldn't be wise to act as if he couldn't stand the smell.

"Mrs. Barnard tells me that you're thinking of investing in the property with the transfer station," Monica said.

They walked toward the main entrance.

"That's right," he said.

In his head, he was thinking about the fact that she had arrived by cab, and the cab driver might have seen him. That definitely ruled out finishing the job today.

"Mrs. Barnard tells me that you work for the government," he said.

They reached the main door, and, ever the gentleman, Larry Evans opened it for her. She smiled. As she passed him, a brief smell of her came to him. It made his stomach lurch. She smelled like peaches.

"Are you okay?" she said.

He had no idea what his face looked like then. Why had she asked?

"Peaches," he said.

"Oh, are you allergic to them? I know my shampoo has a peachy smell, but I don't think you can be allergic to my shampoo unless maybe you were to drink the stuff."

He wasn't really listening to her. There was a buzzing in his head. Then he saw what seemed like a living scarecrow, an elderly woman with no body fat, moving slowly down the hall toward them.

"Ah, Ms. Morgenthau, Mr. Evans. Right on time. Do you care for anything to drink?"

"I'm fine, no thanks," Monica said.

"Mr. Evans, are you all right?" the old lady said.

He found himself staring at her.

"You look like you've seen a ghost," the old lady said. "Doesn't he, Monica?"

As the girl turned toward him, a cloud of peach scent assaulted his nostrils. He closed his eyes.

Man up! He forced himself to open his eyes. He knew he couldn't manage a smile, so he didn't try.

"Must be something I ate," he said.

"You do look a little green around the gills," said the old lady. "Come back to my office, and we'll talk."

She turned and beckoned them to follow her. Larry Evans thought he might gag. He tried to imagine what he was going to do about this. He came up empty.

His mind was a jumble. The aroma brought him back to his childhood. A happy time. He couldn't shake the feeling that he couldn't do his job with the happy thoughts in his head. He couldn't figure out what to do. Do his job? Turn tail and run? As it turned out, he did neither.

Chapter 58

I think that computers have been a real blessing for businesses. The ability to organize, to gather information—priceless.

And the computer at the University of Pennsylvania was my personal blessing, because my friend Barbara was able to tell me within ten minutes that Charlotte Graybolt was an employee of the University. I guess I should add that Barbara enhanced the blessing because she gave me the information, without my having to go to court and obtain a subpoena. She of course swore me to secrecy, saying that I couldn't let anyone know she'd helped me.

I laughed at her. The information was freely available to the Penn community at the University's library. As an alum of the law school, I could have accessed the University's database myself. I was just too lazy to make my way to West Philadelphia, to the campus.

"Thank you, Barbararararah," I said. It was an old joke between us.

Charlotte was the administrator of the undergraduate English department. Barbara had given me her office number. I sat at my desk, staring at the paper on which I'd written the number. Now that I could reach her, what would I say? What if she didn't want to be found? What if my client had lied to me? I closed my eyes and tried to think.

I would give Charlotte the opportunity to explain why she had left England. And to see if she wanted to see her father, after all these years. If she didn't, I'd leave her alone. It seemed like the only right thing to do, ethically speaking. Her father might be unhappy with me, but he wouldn't be the first client who was.

Chapter 59

The old lady was perturbed. Her employee didn't seem very enthusiastic about his job. In fact, he looked depressed. This was not what she expected. She had been assured that he had no compunction about killing women. She feared her plan could fail.

Perhaps she was misunderstanding the look on his face.

"Welcome," she said. "Can I get anyone some coffee?"

"No, thanks." The girl and the man said it at the same time.

"I wouldn't mind some water," the man said. "Just tell me where to find it."

She directed him to the kitchen, the home of the water cooler. She motioned for Monica to sit on the sofa in her office.

"Lovely day, isn't it?" the old lady said. "Warm. I love it when it's warm."

"The aroma from the transfer station is quite noticeable when it's warm," Monica said. "Like today."

The old lady instantly hated her. She did not have her father's social acumen, that was for sure.

The man came into her office. He looked better.

The old lady stopped worrying about the plan failing. Now she couldn't wait until that nasty girl was out of the way. It most likely wasn't going to happen today, but the sooner the better. She wasn't getting any younger.

Chapter 60

I called Charlotte's number, and was rewarded with a live person with a delightful English accent.

I explained who I was. There was a long silence. At least she hadn't just hung up on me. Then I heard her sigh.

"You know, I would just as soon put that part of my life behind me." She laughed. "Of course, it is already behind me. But I'd like to leave it in my past. I'm happy here. I'm applying for citizenship. I have a good job."

"Yes," I said. "I can understand all that. But your father would like to see you again. And as I understand it, you have some money coming to you."

"From my mother," she said. "I know."

"How do you know that?"

"About five years ago I found out she was alive. She wrote to me. I guess she was momentarily lucid. She apologized for what she'd done to me. And told me about the money."

"How did she know where to write to you?"

"Apparently the same way you just helped my father find me. Some private investigator."

"Did you contact her?"

"No. I read the letter, tore it up, and tried to forget it."

I didn't ask her why. Sometimes the past is just too painful to contemplate.

"Any interest in the money?" I said.

"Believe it or not, no. But I also don't want my father to have it. I think I'll donate it to some worthy cause. Can I do that?"

"Of course," I said. "But first you have to accept the money."

"In person?"

"Well, no, I don't think so. You could hire a solicitor in England to handle it for you."

"Perfect," she said. "I'll do that."

"Well," I said, "sorry for your loss."

"It was all so long ago," she said. "But thank you."

"What shall I tell your father?"

"Tell him I'll take the money, but I have no desire to see him."

"I will," I said.

Something told me the news was not going to break my client's heart.

Chapter 61

Larry Evans had his game face on. He nodded. He smiled. He let the two women chatter on about the environmental issues at the transfer station. His gut, however, was churning. What the fuck?

The old lady kept glancing at him as she spoke. Did she sense he was off his game? He stole a glance at the clock sitting behind the old lady's desk. He'd only been here a half hour, but it felt like two years.

"Mr. Evans," the old lady said. "How do you feel about having to clean up the transfer station site?"

He pulled himself out of himself. He remembered the book that gave him his orders. He remembered his lines.

"I'll tell you, ma'am," he said. "I'm disappointed. I thought we'd get some special dispensation from the state."

The girl looked at him then. When she turned her head, he caught a whiff of her hair, the peachy smell. He felt himself going hot, then cold.

"Mr. Evans," said the old lady. "Perhaps the two of you could discuss this aspect of what I hope will be a deal."

"Surely," he said.

He turned to the girl.

"Can you help us make this deal happen? I'd like to go over what we can do and what we can't do. Perhaps over dinner?"

The girl looked angry.

"Mr. Evans," she said, "I don't socialize with the people I'm regulating."

It came out severe. Yet she was a pretty woman. The dissonance struck him. It also struck the old lady.

"Really, Monica, your father would not be as harsh as you are being," she said.

"Mrs. Barnard, I am not my father. I came here today to discuss the issues surrounding a purchase of the transfer station site. It's business. This is not a social event."

"I'd really like it if the federal government could help redevelop this site," he said. "I would think that the mayor, and the governor and even the President would be happy to have something happen here. Don't you?"

He felt better as the lines came back to him. Sometimes it was good to have a script.

The girl narrowed her eyes.

"I don't think the President of the United States is particularly interested in the cleanup of a transfer station in industrial Philadelphia."

"Isn't your job dependent on the President? Doesn't he run the Environmental Protection Agency?"

"Yes, in a way. But the federal government is not as interested in industrial redevelopment as the City of Philadelphia. The EPA is most concerned with the safety and health of our citizens. And cleanup of the environment."

"But surely we can make everyone happy here," said the old lady. "There must be a way."

"Right now, I don't see it," said the girl.

The old lady turned to Larry Evans.

"I'll let you take over from here," she said. "Just no blood in my office, okay?"

She stood up and walked stiffly toward the door.

"Goodbye, my dear," she said. She patted Monica on the shoulder as she passed her.

They both listened to her shuffling steps as she went down the hallway.

"I don't know if she thinks I'm the tough negotiator or you are," Monica said, "but I guess she thinks at least one of us is. If someone's going to draw blood, that is."

Larry Evans took a deep breath.

"Not really," he said. "I'm here to kill you."

Chapter 62

Charles Graybolt wasn't answering his cell phone, so I left a message asking him to call me. I gave him my cell number.

I looked at my watch, and realized that it was almost time to meet Monica for dinner. I just had time for a quick shower and a quick drink.

As I sat at my desk, turning the glass of scotch in my hand, I started a "to-do" list for tomorrow. First on the list was to hire a lawyer to ensure that my transition out of the firm was fair and equitable. Although the idea of grinding my former partners into dust during negotiations appealed to me, I knew that I couldn't do it myself. The old adage says "the lawyer who represents himself has a fool for a client." I didn't want to be the client who's a fool.

Next on the list was to contact Charles if he didn't contact me today.

I tapped my pen several times on my desk. I finished my drink and headed out the door. I was at the restaurant with five minutes to spare. I sat in my car, wondering whether or not to go in. I knew Monica had taken a cab to see Mrs. Barnard. She was just down the street from me. Rather than have her walk in her work finery from her meeting, perhaps it made sense for me to pick her up. In fact, what more could a good father do than to pick up his daughter and take her to dinner?

I turned out of the parking lot toward Barnard Hardware. There were only two cars in the lot, one of which I recognized as Mrs. Barnard's newest white

Cadillac. The other must belong to the suitor for the property across the street. Or perhaps to the owners. In any case, I didn't think Mrs. Barnard would be upset if I appeared. She'd been trying to get me to meet with her for weeks.

I parked the car. I tried the front door of the office. It was, as I'd hoped, open. I headed down toward voices at the end of the hall. Surprise!

Chapter 63

I couldn't believe what I was seeing. Mrs. Barnard was sitting ramrod straight behind her desk. A tall man in cowboy boots had a gun trained on her.

"Jack, thank God," she said.

Without moving the gun, the cowboy glanced quickly at me.

"Nothing to worry about, sir," he said. His voice was soft, with a country twang that I couldn't place.

"Should I call the police?" I said.

I don't know to whom I was talking. Myself, perhaps. Much to my surprise, the cowboy said "yes," and Mrs. Bernard said "no."

"What the hell is going on here?" I said.

"Jack, don't listen to him," she said. "Whatever he says. He's trying to sell you a bill."

It took me a moment to internally translate what she was saying. Mrs. Barnard sometime used expressions from the early twentieth century. I heard Mary Martin in my head, singing "Cockeyed Optimist" from South Pacific: "But every whippoorwill is selling me a bill...." She meant the cowboy was lying, trying to sell me a bill of goods.

I heard footsteps behind me, and swiveled my head as far as I could with the arthritis in my neck. It was Monica.

"What the heck's going on here?" I said.

"Dad!" she said. She gave me a one-armed hug.

"This man was supposed to kill me," she said. "He couldn't do it."

The man cleared his throat. But he didn't speak.

"Mrs. Barnard hired him to kill me," she said.

"What? Why?"

"Jack, this is a mistake," Mrs. Barnard said. "I don't know this cowboy. I don't know why he's here."

Monica rolled her eyes.

"Our current problem," Monica said, "is figuring out what to do about it. This man saved me from this witch instead of killing me. I don't feel really good about handing him over to the police. But I think we need to stop Mrs. Barnard, and if we don't call the police..."

"Ma'am," said the cowboy, "do what you need to do. Don't worry about me."

"Some hitman you turned out to be," Mrs. Barnard said. "Are you sure you killed old Rick and my son? Or was that someone else?"

Now it was Monica's turn to stare. "You did that?" she said.

His gun was still trained on Mrs. Barnard. He said nothing.

His face was blank. Finally, he spoke. He looked at me.

"I'm just a gentleman rancher," he said. "This woman contacted me to tell me about this opportunity to go into business with her. Then she asked me to kill your daughter. Which I wouldn't do."

He looked at me. I stared at him.

"That's your story and you're sticking to it," I said.

"Correct."

Monica started pulling on my sleeve.

"Dad," she said. "Let's talk in the hall for a minute."

I looked at the cowboy. He nodded.

"I'm not going anywhere," he said.

Out in the hall, Monica put her head in her hands and rocked her head back and forth. She took a breath. When she looked up at me, her eyes were shining weirdly.

"Dad, I think he killed those other people."

"I think he's a hired killer," I said.

"He said he couldn't hurt me."

"Maybe he doesn't like killing women."

"According to what the old witch said when he refused to harm me, she hired him because he told her he had no problem killing women."

I looked at my beautiful daughter. Whatever the cowboy had done in his past, something about Monica had touched him. But was that enough reason not to turn him in, along with Mrs. Barnard?

Monica seemed to read my thoughts.

"I know this will sound ridiculous," she said. "But I trust that guy. There's something about him."

I raised my eyebrows.

"He promised me he wouldn't hurt me, no matter what. I believe him."

"I do, I guess. Since obviously he hasn't hurt you yet. But can we turn him loose on the world, knowing what he does for a living?"

"Maybe we can get him to promise not to kill any more people."

"It's how he earns money to live," I said. "Do you think he'd be willing to try some other line of work?"

"I know you're skeptical, Dad, but as you always tell me, you don't know until you ask."

"Why are we whispering in the hall when we could leave this place and call the cops?"

"I don't know," Monica said.

She started back into Mrs. Barnard's office. Instead of running out the door screaming, taking Monica with me, I followed her meekly.

Chapter 64

As the lawyer and his daughter came back into the office, the cowboy turned his head to look at them. He was surprised they hadn't just left the building and called the cops. He watched the old lady out of the corner of his eye. She was old, but she was mean, and he didn't trust her not to do something stupid. He had already checked her desk, and knew she didn't have a gun.

"We have a proposition for you," the girl said.

"You think you can pay him to kill me?" the old lady said. "It won't work. I can always pay him more."

"That's interesting that you thought that," the father said. "Not everyone has people killed, Mrs. Barnard. Did you know that?"

The old lady just stared at him.

The girl came toward the cowboy, and put out her hand.

"Why don't you and my dad talk?" she said. "I'll hold the gun on her."

Larry Evans looked at the young woman, and he handed her the pistol, butt forward.

"Don't trust her," he said.

"I already don't," she said.

He watched in amusement as she took the gun expertly from his hands, and turned it toward the old lady.

"Jesus, Monica," the lawyer said. "What do you know about guns? How do you know about guns?"

"You don't know everything about me, dad," she said. "Go, you two. Talk. Let's see what we can do to get Mrs. Barnard into trouble and our new friend Larry Evans out of it."

Chapter 65

As the men exited the office, Monica glared at Mrs. Barnard. How could she have had her own son killed? What kind of a monster was she?

She was about to say something, but the old woman started first.

"You know, Monica, I've known you your whole life," Mrs. Barnard said.

"And I guess I never knew what a witch you were," Monica said.
"I remember you as being pretty, and vivacious, and fun. Fooled me."

Mrs. Barnard smiled.

"Sometimes, you have to do things for the greater good. In this case, the greater good is my legacy."

"Your legacy as a hag? Your legacy as a craven, heartless killer?"

Mrs. Barnard's face flushed.

"You can't rile me," she said. "You have no idea what I've gone through to get here. I grew up poor. I married to get away from poverty, but then my worthless husband left me. I built this business from scratch, as a single mother raising a son, in a world where only men ran businesses. I got myself an education. My life has been about making something of my self and my work."

Monica moved closer to her, and began a slow figure eight with the gun.

"I'm trying to figure out where to shoot you so that it hurts the most," she said. "You deserve to suffer."

"When you're older, Monica, you'll understand the need to leave something behind."

"You didn't want me to get older," said Monica. "Right?"

Mrs. Barnard was quiet.

Monica stepped closer to the desk, but carefully kept her distance from the old woman's hands.

"You could have left something behind. You could have left your son."

Mrs. Barnard said nothing.

"Do you know how much he suffered when he died? I read about it in the paper," Monica said. "He was killed with one of the most painful poisons that exist. What mother could possibly do that to her child? What the hell is wrong with you?"

Mrs. Barnard screwed her mouth into a grimace. She opened her mouth to speak.

Then all color left her face. She took a gasping breath. She tried to stand, but the effort caused her to fall on her face. She didn't move.

Monica had seen too many television villains try playing dead. She didn't want to approach the witch and have her grab for the gun.
She backed up into the hall, continuing to keep the gun trained on the old lady. Without turning around, she shouted.

"Dad!"

Both of the men came running.

"Are you okay?" her father said. He had turned an unhealthy gray color, the color of worry.

"Yes, I'm fine. It's Mrs. Barnard. She's either a great faker or she had a heart attack. Although heaven knows, she doesn't actually have a heart."

With the two men flanking her, she started walking back into Mrs. Barnard's office. The cowboy picked up his pace, and walked over to the desk. He put his index finger on her neck.

"She's not faking," he said. "She's dead."

"That's perfect," Monica said. "We can all pretend we were never here."

She lowered the gun, and handed it back to the cowboy, butt first.

Her father looked shocked. This whole scene seemed to be too much for him. Monica tried to calm him.

"She wasn't really a person, Dad," Monica said. "She had no heart. She was just a collection of synapses. Now she's not."

The cowboy and her father looked at her.

"I guess I'm not so different from Mr. Evans after all," Monica said. "I hoped that if I baited her enough, she'd die. I figured that was the best way out of this mess. And lest we forget, she tried to have me killed."

Her father was beginning to return to his normal color.

"I certainly was coming up empty," he said.

"I figured I could always shoot her, or something," the cowboy said. "But then I would have had to skedaddle."

He couldn't believe himself. He was talking nonsense.

"You're not going to skedaddle?" Monica said.

"I'm looking to retire," the cowboy said. "Philadelphia seems like a nice city."

He didn't seem to know why he had said that. He looked dazed. Truthfully, he had been thinking for days that he wanted to get out of Philadelphia.

Monica laughed.

"You baby boomers! Dad told me he's retiring. But I can't imagine the two of you becoming golf buddies."

Her father's phone rang. He looked at the phone, but he didn't answer it.

"Let's get out of here," he said. "I'm hungry. Hungry and confused."

Chapter 66

We were sitting in a back booth at the local crab house. It was dark. It was quiet, because the crowds hadn't started to arrive yet. I sat at the table across from my daughter and a cowboy. I had said I was hungry, but really I didn't know what I was feeling. Certainly, something in my gut didn't feel right. We had left a dead woman who used to be my client collapsed at her desk. I felt absolutely no remorse about it, but I felt that I should feel something about it. Something more than what I felt, which was mainly relief.

I looked at my companions.

The cowboy killed people for a living. Yet he had refused to kill Monica. And my dear, sweet daughter, who wouldn't even kill spiders, had knowingly taunted a woman to her death, hoping to induce a heart attack or stroke. My head felt tilted inside.

"What a trip," Monica said. She looked strangely elated.

The cowboy shifted in his seat. He looked uncomfortable.

This new morally uncertain world made me wonder if I really should go back to being a lawyer. Then I thought about the toxicity I had left behind.

"What's going on, Dad? You're thinking deep thoughts. Is it about Mrs. Barnard?"

"Not really. I'm trying to rethink my place in the universe."

I think I might have blushed.

"Sorry. That sounds so grandiose. It's just that I've trained as a lawyer and I've practiced as a lawyer for so many years...my equilibrium feels off. I'm confused. But I know I can't go back to the firm. I really can't stand the fact that working in a firm has become so cutthroat," I said.

I looked at the cowboy.

"To say that about your field is redundant, I guess," I said.

I don't know if I expected him to laugh or smile, but he didn't do either. Luckily, he also didn't kill me. Instead, he surprised me.

"I usually carry out my assignments," the cowboy said. "This time, I didn't. Something's wrong with me. I guess."

He shifted in his chair. He looked at Monica. His eyes searched her face.

Monica flashed me a quick smile edged with triumph. Then the cowboy looked at me.

"I guess I'm confused too. I'm questioning whether I can even do what I'm so good at anymore."

"So if we asked you to stop killing people for a living, you'd stop?" Monica said.

The cowboy looked around, to see who might have heard Monica. But she had lowered her voice. No one had paid any attention. He didn't speak.

"Well, Mr. Evans?" I said.

"I've already stopped," he said. His voice seemed to come through a soupy fog.

"Are you all right?" Monica said.

He shrugged.

"I have no idea," he said.

My phone rang again. It was an international number. I began to have a bad feeling.

I answered the phone. It was Jimmy. Charles Graybolt had gone off the grid. He had checked out of his New York hotel, he'd de-activated his cell phone, and he'd cancelled his return airline ticket. Jimmy thought I should check to make sure Charlotte Graybolt was okay. I hung up the phone.

"I have a situation," I said.

And for some reason, I explained the entire Graybolt situation to my tablemates. Monica listened intently, and the cowboy seemed not to be listening at all until I got to the part about Charles going off the grid. Then he looked at me.

"You better check on the girl," he said.

I scrolled through my cellphone numbers until I came to the one I thought was Charlotte's. I was right, it was her number, but her voicemail picked up. Since it was late in the day, that could mean nothing more than that she had left work.

I called Barbara DuQuesne, my lawyer contact at Penn. Luckily, she worked like a maniac, and she was still in her office.

"Barbara, I might have to ask you for another favor," I said.

"Really?" she said. "I'm shocked."

I sighed. I tried not to sound panicky.

"Barb, I need to get in touch with Charlotte Graybolt. Do you have a cell phone number for her?"

"Jack, what the hell are you bothering me for? I gave you her office number. Didn't you call her?"

"I did. I'm just concerned something might have happened to her."

"What? Why?"

"Her father was looking for her. Now he's disappeared."

"This all sounds very melodramatic," Barbara said. "But it's a nice night, so I'll take a walk over to her office to see if everything's okay. On the way, I'll call the cell number we have on file for her. I'll call you in about ten minutes and let you know. Although I'm sure it's nothing."

"Thanks Barbararararah," I said.

A waiter came over to our table, his wrinkled face a mask of misery. Every line in his face bent down. He threw three menus at us, plopped three sets of napkins, forks and knives in front of us, and gestured toward the bar.

"Drinks?" he said. He was clearly saving his energy.

We all said "just water" at the same time. His pursed lips said it all: he couldn't be bothered with cheapskates. I bet it would be awhile before he returned to take our order. If ever.

"Mr. Evans," Monica said, "what will you do now?"

Again the cowboy shifted in his seat.

"I don't know, long-term," he said.

He turned toward me.

"But I'm thinking short-term you might need some help from me. If that girl is missing. If her father did anything."

"Please don't take this the wrong way," I said. "I'm not suggesting that this is the only way you have of solving problems. But I don't need anyone killed."

He shrugged.

"No offense taken," he said. "But part of my skills involve finding people."

I nodded.

"I'm finding that's not as easy as I'd hoped," I said.

"Then I'm your man," he said.

He moved his chair back from the table, stretched his booted feet out in front of him and folded his arms.

"Well, okay then," I said.

I was discomfited at the idea of working with him, but also relieved to have some professional help. Maybe this would work out.

Then the phone rang, and I reached into my pocket for it with a feeling of panic. It was Barbara.

"Her office is a mess, and there's blood everywhere," she said. "I've called the police."

I began to blubber to her, but she stopped me.

"The police will want to talk to you," she said. "Don't lose your phone. You've gotten me into a world of trouble. Oh, and Jack, you're a dangerous asshole."

She hung up, and I looked balefully at my daughter and my new partner.

"We have work to do," I said.

Chapter 67

The man with the cowboy boots sat in the lawyer's car, in the back seat. His rental car was still in the old lady's parking lot, and he needed to get it out of there. The lawyer agreed to take him to Barnard Hardware.

"Leave me at the gate," the cowboy said. "The less vehicle activity for people to see, the better."

They agreed to meet at the lawyer's house in a half hour. The cowboy watched the lawyer's car turn around, and then he headed for his rental.

His sense of self-preservation caused him to move expeditiously to the car, to get in, and to drive it out of the lot. But he was so rattled by his own behavior, he decided to pull over to try to think clearly.

There was no doubt that something had been happening to him. It wasn't just the girl, although he found himself drawn to her. It was a mental tiredness, an inability to keep himself on track. The thought of going back to his cabin, working on some heavy equipment, and zoning out there should have soothed him, but it didn't.

He checked his watch. He needed to get to the lawyer's house. He might stop doubting himself if he could find the missing girl and her missing father.

Chapter 68

I was making coffee for ourselves and our new friend when Monica sat herself down at the kitchen counter with a deep frown.

"Having second thoughts about playing with a hired killer?" I said.

"Not really, Dad. I guess I figure that if no one is paying him to kill us, we're safe."

I sighed.

"How do we know no one has?"

"Mrs. Barnard wanted him to kill me. He wouldn't. He could have, but he didn't. I think we're safe. Anyway, he said he wasn't going to do that anymore."

"It makes me uneasy," I said. "Or to put it more honestly, having anything to do with him scares the shit out of me."

"Dad! You've never used that kind of language in front of me before."

Monica was shocked, but she was also laughing.

"I'll try not to do it again," I said.

Monica's frown returned.

"It occurred to me that I could turn out to be a suspect in the killings Mr. Evans committed," she said.

"What? That's crazy," I said.

"Crazier than an old lady hiring someone to kill her son and her opponent in a business deal?"

I thought about that.

"I've known Mrs. Barnard for many years now," I said. "If you had asked me if she would kill someone to make her business successful, I would have said yes. But I have to admit, I never would have predicted that she wanted Stanley dead, and that she would have hired the cowboy to do it."

"Maybe we should find out the cowboy's real name," Monica said.

"You know, the police department is in the dark about any murders," I said. "Both the old guy at the transfer station and Stanley looked like accidents. Mrs. Barnard is clearly a natural death. I doubt this is going to come down on anyone."

"Certainly, having the old witch dead puts a period on it," Monica said.

I looked up at the clock over the kitchen window. The cowboy was late. Perhaps he had a moment of clarity, and got the hell out of Philadelphia.

"I feel very guilty about Charlotte Graybolt," I said. "I meddled, and now it seems as though she's missing or hurt, or both."

Monica looked at me, her eyes very serious.

"Dad, you weren't meddling. You were carrying out a job. You did your due diligence, you talked to your friend in England about this Charles guy, you had no way of knowing that anything you did could cause harm."

A soft knock at the front door stopped me from further beating my breast. Monica got up to answer it. I was going to call after her to make sure she knew who it was before opening the door, but I realized how foolish that would be: darling, make sure you only open the door to <u>our</u> hired killer.

The cowboy looked the worse for wear. But I was struck by how ordinary he looked. Brown hair, brown eyes, medium height. Apart from his boots, he was completely unexceptional. Which I guess in his line of work was what came in handy.

"Coffee?" I said.

"Sure."

I poured out three cups, and we all sat at the kitchen table.

"If you give me the name of your client, and the hotel he was staying at in New York, I can probably find out if he's here in Philadelphia."

I wrote the information down on a legal pad.

"Can I use your computer?" he said.

"Okay," I said. I thought briefly about my personal information on my computer, including all my passwords for online banking. It might make sense for me or Monica to join him in my office.

"Feel free to watch over my shoulder," he said, watching my face.

"I've never been good at poker," I said.

I walked into my office with him.

"Just so you know," he said in his soft voice, "I don't steal. I also don't kill unless I'm paid to."

For some reason, he flushed when he said this. He looked me in the eye.

"I once killed someone I didn't have to," he said. "I was drunk. It was a mistake."

"I'm not your priest," I said. "You don't have to confess to me."

He nodded.

He sat at my desk, and moved the mouse to open the internet. He described what he was doing as he was doing it. I was amazed. He had discovered the way in to the database that the airlines and the railroads used to track passengers. He plugged in Charles Graybolt's name. Nothing came up except his cancelled flight to England.

"What if he used a fake name?" I said.

"It would be extremely difficult to do, because since 9/11 everyone has to present identification to buy a ticket for the railroad or the airlines. Unless he knows where to get good fake ids."

"How about on the internet?" Monica said.

She had walked in behind us.

"You can buy a fake license for twenty-five bucks on the internet," she said. "From China. Actually, it was two for twenty-five."

"How do you know that?"

"I bought fake id when I wanted to drink in college and I wasn't 21 yet," she said. She smiled. "Now it can be told."

"Why did you need two?" I said.

"In case a bouncer threw me out and kept the one I used. Then I had a spare for another night."

A faint sound like a muffled chuckle came from our cowboy.

"Jeez, Monica," I said.

"My point," said Monica, "is that Charles Graybolt could have easily found fake id's."

"If he did that," the cowboy said, "Mr. Graybolt would have had to plan in advance that he wanted to travel under an assumed name."

I nodded.

"How about buses?" I said.

"Buses are much easier," he said. "Not the level of scrutiny."

I waited for some further words of wisdom.

"I can get into the Greyhound database," he said. "But all those buses for a buck that go up and down the eastern seaboard—I can't find out about who purchased tickets on them."

He hit a few keys, and shook his head.

"Nothing on Greyhound."

He turned from the monitor to look at Monica and me.

"There's a very time consuming way to try to find him, but I'll need help."

"Call every hotel in the area," Monica said, "and ask to speak to him."

"Yes," he said. "And hope he's not staying with friends."

We divided up the listings on the internet for Philadelphia area hotels. We definitely had our work cut out for us. And if we came up empty, we had the suburban hotels to start on.

It took us five hours, but we did find Charles Graybolt. He was at the Holiday Inn on Walnut Street near the Wanamaker Building. He didn't answer his room phone, though.

We needed to find Charles. Since I'd never seen him, I was banking on his speaking with his English accent. But the cowboy came through again, this time with a photo of Charles pulled from the internet. And now, instead of our fingers doing the walking, we were about to let our legs do it.

Chapter 69

The three of us got into my car. Monica sat in the front with me, the cowboy in the back. Monica put her seatbelt on, and then turned in her seat to the cowboy.

"Is your name really Larry Evans?" she said.

He hesitated.

"No," he said.

"What is your name?"

"You can call me Larry Evans," he said.

"Jeez, it's like Rumpelstiltskin," Monica said. "You think we can't find out your name?"

I looked in the rearview mirror. The cowboy caught my eye. He looked somber.

"Anything is possible," he said. "But I'd rather you didn't."

As we drove to the hotel, I tried to visualize what to expect when we arrived. A police presence? If we could find Charles' whereabouts, surely the police could too. I didn't know many cops. Would Larry Evans be spooked by them?

"Larry," I said. "Will it bother you if there are police at the hotel?"

"I don't know what you mean by 'bother'," he said.

Monica turned to face him.

"You know exactly what he means," she said. "Don't play games."

I was shocked at her forcefulness. I guess the cowboy was too.

"Yes, okay. I'd prefer not to have to deal with them. They'll want me to explain my presence, show i.d., explain how I know you both and how I'm involved in this mess."

I pulled the car over onto the side of the road and shut off the engine.

"Well, Larry," I said, "this is as good a time as any for us to get our stories straight."

Apart from the roaring traffic just feet from our car, you could have heard a pin drop. No one spoke.

Finally, the cowboy shook his head.

"I've been running around like a chicken with my head cut off," he said. "I haven't been thinking. But I can't be with the police just now, because I don't have a cover story. It would take me awhile to create one. Larry Evans won't stand up to scrutiny. My best cover has always been that I'm invisible."

"Do you want us to drop you back at your rental car at Dad's house?" Monica said.

"No," said the cowboy. "I can still help. I just can't present myself as part of your team."

"So you'll be our silent partner," I said.

The cowboy nodded.

"You two meet with the cops," he said. "I'll see what I can find out on my own at the hotel."

"Should we meet someplace at a specific time?" Monica said.

"No," the cowboy said. "You two go wherever you need to go without me. I'll find you if I have any news."

I started the engine and put on my directional, and I merged into traffic with finesse. If I say so myself.

When we arrived at the hotel, I slowed to make the turn into the parking garage, and the cowboy opened the back door of the car.

"I'll be seeing you," he said.

He left the car, and by the time I looked out the window after he slammed the door, I couldn't see him.

Monica looked shocked.

"He's gone," she said. "Do you think we'll see him again?"

I sighed as I waited for the parking lot arm to raise itself.

"Honey, I have no idea," I said.

Chapter 70

I parked our car, willing myself to remember where. Then Monica and I headed for the registration desk. The lobby was crawling with police. I felt faint, possibly for the first time in my life. We walked over toward the scrum. I spied someone in a suit talking to the uniforms. I thought: detective, or reporter? It was a detective, someone I instantly recognized.

"Dolph," I said.

I put my hand on his arm, and he gave me a look that would have shriveled a lesser man. Then he recognized me.

"Jack," he said. "I hear you started this mess."

He wasn't smiling. I began to feel a groan coming out of me, and I squelched it. My daughter inserted herself between us.

"Hi, I'm Monica," she said. "Jack's daughter."

Not surprisingly, Dolph smiled. Most people had that reaction to Monica.

"What can I do to help?" I said.

Dolph looked me in the eye.

"Do you know what this client of yours looks like?" he said.

I pulled out the printed copy of the photo the cowboy had found on the internet. Dolph glanced at it.

"Yes," he said, "we have that, too."

He rolled his eyes and walked away.

"Later, Jack," he said.

"Dad, are you all right?"

I realized that I had pretty much stopped breathing. I took a deep breath.

"Guilt," I said.

"Stop it, now," Monica said.

An officer approached us.

"Excuse me," he said. "We'd like to talk to you, Mr. Morgenthau. Please come with me."

He was very polite. I knew we didn't have to go with him. But my wracking guilt required me to spill my guts, or the beans, or whatever, just to help.

How much could I tell them? How much was I ethically allowed to tell them? What a mess.

Chapter 71

The cowboy was sitting in the hotel coffee shop, searching for a likely candidate. A waitress in a pink dress and a hostess apron came up to his table, and he smiled at her.

"Hi, hon," she said. "Coffee?"

"Yes, please," he said.

He looked into her eyes when he said it. Kept the smile up to full wattage. She blushed.

He relaxed. She would do just fine.

By his second cup of coffee, he had found out from her what all the police activity was about. He had a piece of pie, and was able to elicit the floor of the hotel that had been closed off by the police. He tipped her well, and intimated he would be returning. She blushed again.

She had told him the eleventh floor was the cops' focus. He wandered toward the Sansom Street side of the hotel, where he had seen a freight elevator. It was crowded with cops. He wandered back to the lobby, and strolled toward the elevator bank. Several uniforms glanced at him, but no one stopped him. He entered the first elevator that opened, and hit the "ten" button.

As the elevator began its ascent, he hit "12". When the doors opened at 10, he looked out of the elevator, saw nothing, and got out of the elevator. He walked to the exit stairway. A sign on the door said: "No exit to street. Stairway leads to roof."

He recognized how ludicrous this was, but couldn't stop to ponder it. He stepped through the door and went up the stairs to the eleventh floor. He opened the door slowly, sure he would find a score of cops. He saw two in uniforms in the hallway. He backed out into the stairwell, slowly closed the door, and climbed to the roof level. Always start at the top, he thought.

He again slowly opened the stairwell door, this time to the roof. There was a helipad on top of the building, but no cops. He tested the door to be sure he could exit the way he came in, and stepped out onto the platform. The wind almost knocked him back through the door. The wind was funneling through the buildings, and he briefly wondered how the copter pilots managed to land when the breeze was really blowing.

He paced around the perimeter of the platform, circumnavigating it in ever smaller circles, watching the ground and, occasionally, the door from which he'd come. He thought he saw a drop of blood. He knelt down to get a closer look. It appeared to be one of a series of drops, leading off toward the brick enclosing the platform. He followed them, until they ended at the brick wall. He peered over the edge, and found a brick shelf about five feet below the helipad. On the shelf was a woman, alive, sitting cross-legged, cradling one arm with the other.

"Help me," she said.

He could see her arm was bleeding. Apart from that she appeared unharmed. He jumped down onto the platform.

"Are you the police?" she said.

"No, but I'm here to help you," he said.

"Help my father," she said. "He's in danger. I have to get back to help him."

The cowboy recognized her accent. Definitely British.

"You're Charlotte, right?" he said.

"Yes, and my father is Charles, and I have to help him," she said.

"Can you walk?" the cowboy said.

She nodded, and stood up with a grimace.

"What happened to your arm?"

"Knife," she said. "I couldn't get off of this ledge with only one arm."

The cowboy pulled himself up onto the platform, then lay flat on his stomach and gestured for the girl to approach him.

"I want you to walk up the wall," he said.

He grabbed her under her armpits, trying not to notice her wince of pain. She put a foot on the brick wall, and then another, and then leaned over the cowboy to crawl off the ledge and onto the platform.

"Good job," he said.

She lay on her stomach, and then turned onto her side. He offered his hand, and she stretched out her good arm. He pulled her up into a standing position.

"You need to get to a hospital," he said.

"It's not bleeding so much now," she said. "And my father..."

The cowboy took her good arm and moved her to the door. In the stairwell, he took off his jacket, then his shirt. He took out a small penknife and ripped his shirt into pieces. He made her a bandage of interleaved pieces of shirt. Then he put his jacket back on.

She had said nothing. But a spark lit her eyes.

"Very au courant," she said, nodding at his bare chest. "Very Las Vegas."

"Too bad I don't have a big gold chain," the cowboy said. "Are you ok to walk? Are you dizzy?"

"I'm okay," she said. "My father's room is on the 11th floor."

She began walking down the stairs.

"Anyone in there with him?"

"When I left, a man with a knife was going crazy. He cut me when I tried to get him away from my father."

She was panting a little, but she didn't stop moving.

"Charlotte," he said. "You've got to get the police to help you."

"This hotel is crawling with cops," she said. "It didn't stop this madman. He's holding my father hostage."

"The police have SWAT teams for this very situation," he said.

She sat abruptly on a step, and put her head back. She closed her eyes.

"You've lost too much blood," the cowboy said. "I'll get you to a fire rescue truck outside, and then I'll help your father."

He knelt down, picked her up gently and put her over his shoulder. He carried her down to the tenth floor, exited into the hallway, and headed for the elevators. He wasn't really sure how he could help

Charles Graybolt. But he knew Charlotte needed medical attention, and he would make sure she got it.

Chapter 72

The lobby of the Holiday Inn is not large. As a result, I felt claustrophobic and anxious. We were surrounded by people who were pissed off at me, and I certainly felt the bad vibes.

The door opened on one of the elevators, and Larry Evans stepped out carrying a woman. Monica and I converged on him at the same time, but he kept walking toward Walnut Street.

The woman was pale but breathing. Her arm was bloody, and I realized that the makeshift bandage was from the cowboy's shirt.

"It's Charlotte," he said. "She was stabbed. Her father's in danger from the same fruitcake. I'm taking her to a Fire Rescue truck."

He carried her out the door to the Fire Rescue team waiting outside the garage entrance. The team galvanized into action, taking Charlotte from him and heading for their truck. As soon as we saw the team put her on a stretcher, Larry Evans backed away and turned to me.

"I'm going back in there," he said. "You tell the EMTs about Charlotte."

I started to protest, but he was gone. I put my arm around Monica, and we walked over to the truck.

"I feel guilty saying this," I said, "but I'm relieved that Charlotte wasn't stabbed by her father."

"So you relieved your guilt by feeling guilty about something else?" Monica said.

I laughed a little.

As we approached the truck, a police officer tried to move us away.

"That young lady is Charlotte Graybolt," I said. "Her father is my client. I'm a lawyer."

I reached into my pocket to display my Pennsylvania Bar card, but the cop waved me toward the truck.

"I thought you weren't a lawyer anymore, Dad," Monica said.

I sighed.

Charlotte was sitting up, although several EMTs were trying to make her lie down. There was an IV in her arm, and an oxygen mask on her face. She was saying "my father" in a loud but muffled voice.

"Charlotte, I'm Jack Morgenthau, your father's lawyer," I said.

She stopped talking.

"Have you told the police what's going on with your father?"

She shook her head.

"Can you talk?"

She nodded.

"Monica, honey," I said, "would you go get Dolph for me?"

"He doesn't know me," she said. "I'll stay with Charlotte. You go get him."

She smiled at Charlotte and gave me a little shove.

As I walked back into the hotel lobby, I saw the cowboy exit one of the elevators. He made a beeline for me.

"He's no longer in danger," he said. "And I have to get out of here. I'll take a cab."

He kept his head down and kept walking, leaving by the Walnut Street door. He turned toward Broad Street.

And then Dolph was in front of me, and he grabbed me by my arms.

"What is it about you, Jack, that draws…issues, let's say."

Dolph was beginning to sound like my former law partners.

"Do you mind telling me what you're talking about?" I said.

"Your client, Charles Graybolt? He's alive, and talking. And he says he didn't hurt his daughter."

"Where is he? How did you find him? And I know he didn't hurt his daughter. She's over with the EMT's on the garage side of the entrance."

He dropped my arms and started walking toward the truck.

"Wait a minute," I said.

I grabbed his arm.

"Stop and talk to me, Dolph."

"Did you know that old lady client of yours, Mrs. Barnard, is dead?"

"What?"

I don't know if my dramatic reading was good enough, but Dolph seemed to buy it.

"Found by her daughter-in-law about an hour ago. Died at her desk. Heart attack."

"Geez, that's awful," I said. "At least she died with her boots on, huh?"

"I don't even know what that means," Dolph said. "But an awful lot of your clients are collecting troubles around them."

I started to protest, but he drew me along with him toward the truck and Charlotte and Monica.

"You have some 'splainin' to do," he said over his shoulder.

And I thought: you have no idea. But that's not what I said.

"I don't owe you any explanation about the Graybolts," I said.

He paid no attention to me. Instead, he pulled aside one of the EMTs, and started getting a health update on Charlotte. Monica saw me and walked over.

"Do you have any idea what's happening?" I said.

"Charlotte said she and her father were having a terrific talk, really coming to an understanding, in her office, when an old boyfriend attacked them both with a knife."

"What? Really? Why?"

"Charlotte says she had a restraining order against him. He saw her talking to her father and went ballistic. She says the guy probably thought her father was a new boyfriend or something."

"That's pretty crazy," I said.

"Her father whisked her into his rental car, and they headed for the hotel. They almost made it into his room when the crazy boyfriend showed up and pushed them into the room. Charlotte escaped while he was knifing her dad."

"Why didn't they call the cops?"

Monica threw up her hands.

"I never got that far with her, Dad."

"This is cockamamie."

Dolph headed for us, and heard my comment.

"If cockamamie means what I think it does, you're right," he said. "Did you know we found a wounded man and a dead man in Mr. Graybolt's room?"

Monica and I stole a quick glance at each other.

"Which one was Mr. Graybolt?" I said.

"The wounded guy," he said, and pointed out a stretcher being removed from the elevator. Two EMTs holding IV bags were wheeling it.

"He's breathing," Dolph said. "Going in and out of consciousness."

"Is he going to make it?" Monica said.

"According to the EMTs, he will."

Dolph looked at me.

"I'd like to know how a man as badly wounded as Charles Graybolt could manage to break the neck of his attacker. Since he's your client, I thought you might have some insight."

I shook my head.

"Sorry," I said. "Not a clue."

I put my arm around Dolph.

"Sorry to see you in these circumstances, Dolph, but it was good seeing you. I'm taking my daughter home, now, so we can have a much needed drink."

He just stared as I shook his arm and turned away, Monica at my side. I wondered if Larry Evans would be at my house, or if we had seen the last of him.

We took the parking garage elevator, and it only took us two or three tries before we found my car. I decided it was a metaphor for my life. Eventually, I succeed.

Chapter 73

The man with the cowboy boots checked out of his hotel. He turned in his rental car a block away. He carried his suitcase down Delaware Avenue until he saw a cab. He waved it over. He asked to be taken to the bus terminal. He thought of the man he'd killed in the hotel, a man whose name and motivation was completely unknown to him. Not so different from his usual assignments.

At the terminal, he paid the driver. He looked around at Philadelphia's Chinatown, and its sadly deteriorated mall. He watched an ambulance race by, its lights flashing and its siren wailing. He was looking forward to his peaceful respite at his ranch.

He walked to the ticket counter, trying to ignore the stench of urine and rotting food, and paid for a ticket out of town. He strolled over to the bus parking area. He tried to will himself out of his feeling of dejection.

And then he gave up. He pulled out his cell, and called a number he had memorized without realizing it.

Chapter 74

When Monica and I got home, I discovered I was disappointed that Larry Evans was not there. The last twenty-four hours with him had made be realize that he could be useful to me in my new profession as an investigator. On the other hand, hanging out with a contract killer was scary as hell.

"That's too bad," Monica said.

We had just walked into the kitchen.

"What is?" I said.

"He's not here," she said.

I nodded.

"I began to feel as though he was some sort of protector," she said.

"I want a scotch," I said, "and I'd like to find out what the hell is going on with Charles Graybolt."

Monica opened a bottle of wine for herself, and I poured a generous amount of Glenfiddich in a glass without ice. I headed for the phone. I called Dolph. Then I sat at my desk chair while several layers of operator shunted me around from office to office. Finally I reached him.

As he did the last time I'd seen him, he gave me a hard time over my clients' unfortunate tendencies to get into trouble, get hurt, or die. I couldn't deny how peculiar it was, for me as well. For the many years I'd worked as a lawyer, none of my clients had died, until this year.

When he finally stopped ragging on me, he gave me some information.

"Your client, Mr. Graybolt, he's at Jefferson Hospital. He's going to make it. Lost a lot of blood, but he's going to be okay. The guy who stabbed him, some freak who was obsessed with his daughter."

"Is Charlotte okay?"

"Yeah, she's going to be fine, too. Thirty stitches in her arm, but the nut case missed any major blood vessels."

"What the hell happened?" I said.

"Turns out the freak used to be her boyfriend. Then he started becoming violent. She took out a restraining order. But he was too fucked up. He shadowed her at work, saw her with her father, and pulled out a knife. His attack started at her office, made its way to his hotel."

"Wow," I said.

"Yeah," he said. "And here's something even stranger. The girl claims she has no idea how her father broke the guy's neck. The EMTs told me there was a guy who took her most of the way to their truck, but she says she doesn't remember any guy. Do you?"

"No," I said.

"I can't figure out if this is related to your other two clients dying," he said. "Mrs. Barnard and her kid."

"It's not related," I said.

"I hope not, Jack," he said.

He hung up.

I glanced at my glass, sorry to see the liquid completely gone. I went for some more. I relayed the story to Monica.

Her cellphone rang. She had left it on my desk. I grabbed it. The number was blocked. I had a feeling. I guess she did too.

"Answer it, Dad," she said.

"Hello?" I said.

There was a brief moment of silence on the other end, and then a familiar voice spoke.

"I wasn't expecting you to answer her phone," the cowboy said. "But I wanted you both to know my number, in case you need anything."

He rattled it off, and I grabbed a pen, wrote it down, and read it back to him.

"You got it," he said.

"Where are you?"

"On a bus back home," he said.

"Oh," I said.

We were both quiet. I couldn't think of anything to say. Monica grabbed the phone from my hand.

"Mr. Evans," she said. "Be safe."

She turned off the phone, and went back to the kitchen to pour more wine into her glass.

Turn the page for a bonus preview, the beginning of the next story in the Odd Fellows series: A Taste of Paradise

Odd Fellows:

A Taste of Paradise

By Janet Kole

"An Odd Fellow bases his thoughts and actions on healthy philosophical principles. He believes that life is a commitment to improve and elevate the character of humanity through service and example. He is humble in a way that he never boasts about himself. He knows and accepts his strengths and weaknesses and keeps away from badmouthing people and making unreasonable allegations. He understands that certain things in life are unavoidable. He is aware of the vanity of earthly things, the frailty and inevitable decay of human life and the fact that wealth has no power to stop the sureness of eventual death. He then asks the question, "How am I going to spend my life?""

Source: The Independent Order of Odd Fellows, IOOF website.

This is a work of fiction. Any resemblance of the characters to real people, living or dead, is purely coincidental.

The Philadelphia I describe is not wholly realistic. I've made some changes to the geography to facilitate the story.

Any legal issues that arise in this story are simplified and so not completely accurate. Also, as most lawyers know, the law changes so quickly it can make your head spin. As for the practice of law I describe, as practiced in a big firm, it is only a slight exaggeration.

The name "Odd Fellows" arose because, in smaller towns and villages, there were too few Fellows in the same trade to form a local Guild. The Fellows from a number of trades therefore joined together to form a local Guild of Fellows from an assortment of different trades, the Odd Fellows.

Wikipedia

Preface

Dane Andrews and his caddie finished their lagers and headed out the door of the waiting area onto the tarmac. Dane loved owning an airplane. He admired the sleek fuselage, and his "vanity" tail number, N25DA. The "25" was how old he was when he won his first major golf tournament.

The pilots of his jet were going through their final preflight check, and Dane wanted to take off as soon as possible, to get home to Philly. Dane's wife was holding a 60th birthday party at the Barclay Hotel for him, and he didn't want to be late.

Dane went first. He was halfway to his seat when his caddy lurched into the side of the door to the plane. Dane shook his head. He spoke to the flight attendant.

"No more for Morrell," he said. "He's obviously had enough. Coffee and a snack, but no booze."

The caddy turned to face Dane.

"Fuck you," he said.

He turned and left the plane.

"Hey, Morrell," Dane said.

He rose from his seat and walked to the door, and started back down the steps to the tarmac.

"Morrell, we need to leave," he said.

The caddy was almost back at the flight facility. Dane had to shout to be heard.

"Morrell, turn around now or we're going without you."

Morrell turned, but it was only to raise his middle finger at Dane.

Dane turned back, and walked up the steps. He hated to leave Morrell without transportation, but he hated the thought of missing his party more.

Dane turned into the cockpit.

"Wheels up," he said. "We're not waiting for that asshole."

The pilots nodded, and laughed a little.

Dane buckled himself in as the attendant closed the door and the engines began to rev. As soon as they took off, Dane was fast asleep. The attendant, sitting in her jump seat, smiled at the man. He was certainly a creature of habit. Out like a light as soon as they were in the air.

One of the pilots poked her head out of the cockpit door.

"We're almost at our cruising altitude," she said. "We'll put it on autopilot, and then we'll have a snack."

"You got it," the attendant said.

It wasn't long before there was utter silence in the cabin and the cockpit. It happened slowly. They didn't know they were dying. The windows began to ice over. No one snacked. No one spoke. No one was alive.

Chapter One

Let's talk about feelings. My feelings. Every time I say "I'm not a lawyer anymore," I smile. I feel my muscles unwind. I've been out of my law firm only a few months, but not being there anymore still tickles me and makes me insanely happy.

My new venture is to try to help people investigate things or fix things, both of which I did for clients when I was a lawyer, for thirty years and up until just a few months ago. My daughter Monica, a government lawyer, helps me. And we have a partner whom we see only when we need him. He used to be a contract killer. He's about my age and, like me, he's "retired." We don't know his real name, but he says we can call him Larry Evans. We have his cell number. We have no idea where he lives.

One of the things I can do now that I'm my own boss is to play music all day. Another is to take golf lessons. And of course, wait while word gets out that I'm available, just not as a lawyer anymore. I'm waiting for word of mouth to get my business going. In the mean time, I'm doing all the things I always told myself I'd do when I'm retired.

I sat down at my computer to check on what was going on in the world. One unexpected piece of bad news was that my old college buddy, Dane Andrews, had died in a crash of his own airplane. He was on his way from a golf tournament back here to Philly for his 60th birthday party.

What a tragedy. He left behind his sweet wife and two nice kids.

Dane was a pro golfer from Philadelphia, and he and I went to college together at Penn. I knew his wife Penny Andrews from when the two first started going steady. When I felt like assaulting my ego, I'd play a friendly round of golf with Dane. Once he turned pro, I stopped that nonsense. But we still occasionally got together for dinner.

The article on the website of the Inky (what we Philly natives call the Philadelphia Inquirer) was short on details. I was shaking my head when my phone rang. It was Miles Sawyer, a wonderful Philly lawyer to whom I had often referred clients when I had a conflict of interest. He was now representing me in negotiations with my

former law firm to get a return of my capital and various
and sundry other amounts of money they owed me.

"What's going on?" I said.

"I'd like to tell you I got you all your money, but I'd
be lying," he said.

"Did you get anything?"

"Not yet," he said. "We have to play this out. You
know how lawyers are."

"So..." I said.

"I'm actually calling you with some work for your
new venture."

I smiled.

"Great," I said. "For pay?"

Miles laughed.

"I thought you told me you were well off and didn't need the money from the firm, you just wanted it as a matter of principle."

"True," I said. "But I've discovered that people who pay me value what I do more than people who don't."

"Well, this is a very well off paying client. I just don't know if you can help her, because she's on what I think is an unrealistic quest."

"Okay, you have me salivating," I said.

"It's Penny Andrews, Dane's wife. Well, I guess widow."

"Yes, I just saw the news. I thought you and your law firm represent the family?"

"This is more non-lawyer work," he said. "She thinks Dane's death wasn't an accident."

I was speechless.

"Penny thinks someone brought the plane down on purpose. She thinks it was murder."

I agreed to talk to Penny. I thought it was improbable that someone would bring a plane down to murder one person on it. But it turned out that she was right.